THE STYX

JONATHON KING

OPEN ROAD

INTEGRATED MEDIA

NEW YORK

copyright © 2009 by Jonathon King

ISBN: 978-1-4532-0990-5

Published in 2010 by Open Road Integrated Media
180 Varick St.
New York, NY 10014
www.openroadmedia.com

CONTENTS

CHAPTER ONE

ALWAYS THE WOMEN CAME FIRST. ONCE they knew it was safe, that it wasn't something contagious, that there wasn't something violent still flying around: bullets, blades, fists. When it was a so-called natural death, the women were the first at the door, tapping lightly and calling out the name of the son.

"Michael? Michael, luv? It's Mrs. Ready from down the way. Come to help you. Please now. Open up and let us in, lad."

When death befell one of their own, someone like them, the word would pass through the slum more quickly than a gutter fire. And when it was another woman, a peer, an Irish mother, it was like a looking glass of their own inevitable demise, and Jesus, Mary and Joseph, it had to be put together in the way only a woman could.

Michael got up from the straight-back chair and went to the knocking at the door without turning his head from his mother's face, like she might still awaken and bark a command or call out: "Aye, who's it now?"

He had been staring at her dusty profile for only an hour or so now, ever since the local doctor had pronounced her dead and walked back down the tenement stairs. It was not like the vigil he'd sat for the three days she'd laid there, her cough rattling in her tiny chest like broken glass in a paper bag, sweat pouring off her brow in such gouts he swore the wet cloth he dampened from the washbasin was itself drawing the perspiration from her skin. The rag would go on cool and damp and come away hot in his hands as he rung it out.

"It's a fever, mama, it'll break soon," he'd kept repeating.

"I know it will, Danny. I know. I'll be up in a bit, son. Just a bit." She'd mistaken him for his older brother, the one who'd left.

But they were the very same words she'd said to him for as long as he could remember when it was he in the bed with the croup or that one winter with pneumonia. She was his mother, always there. But now she was thirty-nine, ten days from forty, and he was twenty-three. It was a role reversal that would have seemed surreal but for the reality of the pain that tore at him.

"She's gone now, Michael," the doctor had said to him at dawn. "Gone to the Lord, bless her soul."

He'd listened, without taking his eyes away from his mother's face, as the doc packed his bag, closed the door behind him, and clomped down the narrow staircase in his old shoes. How many journeys does that man make a day on these tenement steps, where the denizens of the Lower East Side fall every hour, like grains of sand, only to be replaced by another wave of immigrants washed ashore? What's the Lord got to do with it?

And then the women came. Michael answered the tapping, stared out at Mrs. Ready and a tight clutch of others; he recognized Mrs. Brennan, his best friend's mother, and Mrs. Phelan, from above the bakery, and another he barely knew. They were bundled in winter coats and dark hats and were carrying baskets the contents of which only they knew.

Mrs. Ready stepped into his space and looked up into his eyes, and for the life of him he didn't know how to react. The woman, not much older than his own mother, put her palms to his cheeks. "We know you're hurtin', Michael. But let us do what needs doin'. Go downstairs now to the street and get some air, lad."

He watched the others move in, sliding immediately to the bedside, dark hens come to cluck and perhaps to weep over another. When Michael said nothing and just stood with the door open, staring, Mrs. Ready came back to him, picking up his coat on the way and draping it over his shoulders.

"Go on now. We'll find our way," she said and gently ushered him out.

Outside it was barely eight a.m. and the street unusually full. Michael stood on the steps of their tenement and looked about as if he hadn't lived in the building for most of his life. These were the streets where he and his father had walked hand in hand on Saturday mornings to the poultry shop on Pitt Street.

The once-a-month chicken had always been Michael's choice. Then his father was gone. These were the streets where he and his brother had chased and been chased by a dirty flock of Irish kids, dodging the wagons, scrapping after spilled produce, finding ways to entertain themselves, be it a stickball game or gawking at some irrelevant gang fight. Then Danny was gone. These were the streets where his mother had a magical touch for finding the deals for food and bartering for work and cajoling a city worker for word of an inoculation program or infestation warning, all the things that kept them alive. And now she was gone too. "You're going to watch me die of a broken heart," she'd told him three days ago through lips cracked with the heat of her fever. "Don't let anyone tell you it can't happen, m'boy. Aye, it's a sure malady when you lose your husband and your son."

"You haven't lost your son, Mama," Michael told her. "Danny's coming home when he finds his treasure, and I will always be here with you."

Now the street scene seemed unrecognizable as he stood with his hands in his pockets, eyes reddened from grief and lack of sleep and mind gone so numb he didn't hear the man in front of him until the elder fellow took his sleeve.

"Michael! Michael Byrne," the man was saying. "It's me, James Brennan, Jackie's father."

Michael shook his head while Mr. Brennan was shaking his hand, and both actions seemed to pull him back to reality.

"Sorry, Mr. Brennan. Sorry, sir. I was just—"

"Don't even say it, lad. We're the ones'er sorry for the loss of your dear mother. Jackie told us how sick she was and all."

The elder man had looped his arm through Michael's, as a gesture of both moral and physical support, considering his dazed state. The morning air was still near freezing, and Michael had been just standing there on the stoop, staring out at the cold dankness of the city.

"We've already taken up a bit of a collection, Michael. We've got a coffin maker from Hanlon's, and we'll get the wagon arranged for three this afternoon," Mr. Brennan was saying. "It'll be a fine send-off, lad. No worries now, OK?"

Michael watched a coal wagon creak by in the street, pulled by a haggard old mare, tired before the day had even begun.

"A wagon?"

"Aye, out to the cemetery over in Brooklyn, son," Mr. Brennan said. "Unless you've got other plans. Maybe a special arrangement with St. Brigid's?"

Michael hadn't been to St. Brigid's in ten years. His mother had been devoted to the old famine church on Avenue B, a rock for Irish immigrants like themselves. But she stopped going to services after Michael's father had gone and instead took to cursing her religious tenets on a regular basis, blaming God for leaving her damned and in the grips of hell over the last few years. Cemeteries in the city had been banned years ago as land became scarce. The rural fields of Brooklyn had become the resting place for the modern dead.

"Uh, no, sir. No, the wagon is fine, sir. Thank you, sir."

The two stood there together, watching out over the street, Mr. Brennan stamping his feet in the cold, Michael blinking his eyes as if taking shutter photos of a world he didn't recognize anymore. On several occasions men or women with faces he should have known came up and offered their condolences. The men shook his hand, clasping it with both of theirs as though he'd come through some sort of initiation of pain into their world of adulthood. The women simply took his hands in theirs and looked into his glossy eyes with a knowledge he had never seen before.

Yes, his father was gone, but there had never been condolences given like these. Yes, his older brother had left, but it was an absence of his own making, a choice even. Now Michael was the only one left, a position that harbored this sympathy in others but only froze Michael for now.

"Ah, there, boy. The ladies are finished," Mr. Brennan finally said and turned Michael back to his own entryway. The four ladies were descending the steps, moving in a dark pack. Again Mrs. Ready took his hands.

"She's ready, son," the woman said. "If you'll just sit with her now, we'll start spreading the word and you can greet the well-wishers. We'll make sure you get some food in you, too, Michael."

She then turned to Mr. Brennan.

"The wagon has been arranged?"

"Aye. Three o'clock."

She patted Michael on the sleeve. "We'll be back, son. You won't have to do this alone."

When they'd gone, Michael made his way back up into his flat. Lying on the bed, his mother's corpse had been transformed. The women had found her black dress, had apparently spongebathed her and changed her clothing. They'd used some kind of scented water. The room smelled of flowers instead of sweat and mold and sickness. They'd left two extra kerosene lamps to help brighten the room. All had been carefully posed: his mother lying square in the middle of the bed, her black church shoes buffed and tied, her dress unwrinkled and tucked just right along her thin body. Her hands were folded on her chest, the fingers interlaced, the ring his father had given her before they even left Ireland on her finger and turned prominently upward. Her eyes were closed, and the grimace of death had been replaced by simple manipulation of skin going slowly into rigor. The women had used perhaps their own makeup to cover her mottled gray face and had added just a whisper of rouge. Still, when Michael looked down at his mother, her face seemed to be melting; the bones of her cheeks and nose looked as if they would expose themselves as her skin slackened. The women had added some color to her lips to keep them from going dark, but even with the faux stoicism they placed on her face, she seemed a puttied version of herself.

Michael washed himself and dressed in the best clothes he had, a pair of corduroy pants, a shirt that could still pass for white, and a threadbare jacket. He took up his post in the straight-backed chair again and listened for the inevitable sound of footsteps up the stairwell.

The Sheehans from the butcher's shop down the block came. The Huntaways from next door. The Flannigans from the tavern. Couples his mother's age that he barely knew came and pressed coins rolled in pieces of cloth into his hand. Women brought pots of stew and sweetbreads and placed them on the only table in the room. Three young boys came with flowers. Michael didn't know their names. "They went out and got them from the professor up on Tenth Street who grows a garden," their father said. Michael nodded. He and Danny had done the same when they were that age and old Mrs. Clancy died, but he didn't remember them asking first. He caught himself wondering if it was from the same garden. So long ago.

Near the end of the prescribed two hours of visitation, one of Danny's old friends showed up. Ian Cronin. Ian and Danny had been thicker than thieves until Cronin had joined the police.

"Aye, Michael," Cronin said, taking Michael's hand. "Heard about yer mum. Sorry." Cronin was an officer up in midtown, and Michael kept the surprise out of his eyes. He hadn't seen Cronin since long before Danny disappeared, and even though he and Michael had both been officers back then, they rarely crossed paths. Cronin's head was lowered, maybe in reverence to the moment, but Michael had a sense that Cronin was hesitant to look him in the eye.

Still, Cronin did the dutiful thing, stepped up to the bed where Michael's dead mother lay and made the sign of the cross and then knelt and whispered a blessing. Then he stood and turned to Michael and took his hand again, but this time there was an envelope in his palm.

"Sorry again, Michael," he said. "I should have come sooner."

Michael looked at him quizzically but only nodded and folded the envelope into his pocket.

Afterward, the women stepped forward again, gathered together the food and then took Michael by the elbow and escorted him down the staircase. Four men with tools in their hands and slats of fresh-hewn pine under their arms passed them going up.

Michael ate out on the stoop, barely tasting the food. The women kept passing plates to him and then reloaded each time he refused more. As he ate he could hear the tapping of nails upstairs and the low voices of the men singing an Irish dirge that he could not place.

At one o'clock an empty wagon pulled by two unmatched horses clattered up to the curb. As if that was their signal, the men from upstairs carried the coffin down the stairs and slid it carefully into the back. Also on that seeming signal, some two dozen people from the neighborhood queued up along either side of the wagon. Jonas Ready stepped up next to Michael and, with the tact of a fine waiter, got him up and positioned behind the jury-rigged hearse. From the inside of his coat pocket Mr. Ready withdrew a flask that he passed to Michael. The whiskey went down like a jolt but could not bring a tear to Michael's eyes. The long night and morning had done that, and he had nothing left. He took another long swig to be sure, and then Jonas Ready gave the wagon driver a tip of his hat and the entire ragtag procession began, more tactful and reverent, stoic and proud, hopeful and helpful to the memory of Michael Byrne's mother than its members ever were when she was alive.

CHAPTER TWO

SHE TOOK THE NEWS OF IT from the night air, in the odor of hot pine sap bubbling as the trees burst into flames and in the smell of dry plank wood charring in fire. She stood on the back porch of the luxurious Palm Beach Breakers overlooking the ocean and turned her face to the north, and the scent on the breeze furrowed her brow.

"What is it, Miss Ida?"

The young woman had picked up on the look in Ida's face. She was perceptive that way, unlike others of her kind. It was why Ida liked the girl. But though she might be good at detecting emotion in the careful faces of the hired help, the girl did not have a nose for burning wood floating on salt air. The old woman did not turn to the girl's question and instead kept her head high and her eyes focused on the treetops at the dark northern horizon, searching for a flickering light. She drew in another deep breath for confirmation and then began to move off the painted steps of the hotel.

"Miss Ida?" the young woman said. Her long dress rustled as she hurried down to catch up. "What is it?"

The old woman was still scanning the trees, her eyes showing only a hint of anxiety, but the girl could see moisture welling in them.

"I'm sorry, ma'am," Ida May Fleury said without breaking stride, "but I believe they are burning my home."

The two women walked quickly down the broad walk and around the northern side of the hotel: Ida May Fluery, the head housekeeper at the Breakers, and Marjory McAdams, daughter of a Florida East Coast Railway executive. The one in the lead was a small black woman in a dark work dress with a white apron to mark her employment. Folds of her skirts were in her fists, and her hard leather shoes were flashing across the crushed rock of the service road. Struggling to keep up, Marjory McAdams was also in a dress, but one of considerable fashion and not made for running. Thom Martin, one of the Breakers' bellmen, was smoking under the hotel's portico when he took note of them and would have been quite willing to watch the younger woman's ankles as she hiked her dress to keep pace until he recognized who she was and the direction both were heading.

"Miss McAdams," he called out as he ditched the cigarette and hustled after them. "Uh, Miss McAdams, ma'am?"

Neither of the women turned to him until he had run to catch up and again called out Marjory's name.

She finally spun to him and appeared surprised, but turned instantly in control. "Mr. Martin. Fetch us a calash, quickly, please. We need to take Mizz Fluery home." She kept moving with the older woman.

The bellman stopped jogging but still had to lengthen his walking stride to keep up with them. He hesitated at the request but had to consider it, coming as it was from a superior's daughter.

"Uh, ma'am, there's no one down in the Styx tonight, ma'am," he said, trying to be pleasant and deferential. "They're all across the lake at the festival, ma'am. I, uh, could get a driver to take you all over the bridge to West Palm."

The elderly woman had yet to either acknowledge the bellman or slow her stride. But Marjory McAdams snapped her green eyes on the man and sharpened her voice:

"Either get us a calash, Mr. Martin, or I shall fetch one and drive it myself, and you know, sir, that I am quite capable."

The bellman whispered "shit" as the women continued on, and then he turned and ran back toward the hotel.

They were already onto the dirt road leading through the pines and cabbage palms to the northern end of the island when the thudding sound of horse hooves and the rattle of harness caught up to them. Marjory had to take Miss Fluery by the elbow to pull her to the side as Mr. Martin slowed and stopped next to them. Without a word they both scrambled up into the calash before the bellman had a chance to get out and help. As they settled in the back, he turned in his seat:

"Miss McAdams, please ma'am. All of us was asked to stay out of the Styx tonight. It might be best..."

"Mr. Martin, can you now smell that smoke in the air?" Marjory said, meeting his eyes. Martin turned to look into the darkness, even though the odor of burning timber was now unmistakable.

"Yes, ma'am," he answered, without turning back to face them.

"Then go, sir."

"Yes, ma'am," he said and snapped the reins.

The horse balked at the darkness with only the light of a three-quarter moon to guide it, but it moved at the driver's urging. Miss Fluery kept her eyes high and forward and could see the gobs of smoke that caught in the treetops and hung there like dirty gauze. In less than another quarter-mile, she stood up with a grip on the driver's seat, and Marjory could see the new set of the woman's jaw. She too could see flickers of orange light coming through the trees as if from behind the moving blades of a fan. Despite his reluctance, Mr. Martin urged the horse to speed.

"It may only be a wildfire," Marjory said carefully, but the old woman did not turn to her voice of hope as they pressed on.

Minutes later the carriage slurred in the sandy roadway when they rounded a final curve and came to a full stop at the edge of the clearing. The horse reared up in its traces and wrenched its head to the side as the heat of some two dozen cones of fire met them like a wall, and the white, three-quarter globe of the animal's terrified eye mocked the moon.

Marjory had been to the Styx before, having talked Miss Fluery into letting her walk the distance to see some new baby the housekeeper had described. Marjory knew she was defying all social rules, but her inquisitiveness had long been a part of her character. The Styx was the community where all the Negro workers—housemaids, bellhops, gardeners and kitchen help—lived during the winter season, when the luxurious Royal Poinciana and the Breakers were filled with moneyed northerners escaping the cold.

Marjory had not been shocked by the simple structures and lack of necessities in the Styx. She was not so naïve and sheltered in her family's mid-Manhattan enclave not to have witnessed poverty in New York City. She had seen the tenements of the Bowery and had secretly had her father's driver, Maurice, take her through the infamous intersection of Five Points to witness the sordid and filth-ridden world of the Lower East Side.

The Styx was, by comparison, quaint, she had justified. The shacks of the workers were made of discarded wood from the Poinciana's construction and slats from furniture crates and shipping cartons. Some were roofed in simple thatch made with indigenous palm fronds, others in sturdier tin. Miss Fluery had told her that two winters ago, one of Flagler's railcars had jumped the small-gauge tracks to Palm Beach Island and collapsed into splinters as it rolled down the embankment to the lake. Given permission, the black workers had scavenged the debris, and the car's tin roof ended up covering six new homes in the Styx.

On this night the thatch roofs had become little more than cinders floating up on hot currents into the air. The tin ones were warped and crumpled by the heat like soggy playing cards. As the women and driver watched, the Boston House rooming home fell in on itself, sending up a shower of glowing embers and a billow of dark smoke.

Ida May had not loosened her grip on the driver's iron seat handle and had not turned her face away even as the heat scorched her old cheeks. Marjory put her hand on the woman's arm.

"Mr. Martin said everyone has gone across the lake to the fair, Miss Ida. Surely no one was at home. Surely they're all safe."

Fluery looked into the flames of her home, which had stood at the prominent crown of the makeshift cul de sac and listened to the sound of clay bowls shattering in the heat and ceramic keepsakes exploding into hot dust. She did not acknowledge the girl's words. Marjory was a young white lady from the North. She could not discern the smell of linen and Bible parchment burning any more than she could recognize the odor of charred flesh. But Ida May Fluery knew that smell. The news of death was already in the air.

No, they surely are not all safe, Ida thought. And just as surely, she thought, whoever it is, someone has murdered them.

The rest of Ida May's neighbors would hear the news by word of mouth, and it was as rapid and frightening and as unpredictable as the flames themselves.

Mr. Martin rattled back through the woods at an axle-breaking speed to the hotel as much to report the fire as to pull someone of more importance into the situation. He left Miss McAdams and the old house woman at the edge of the burning shantytown. They had refused to budge when he begged them to come back with him, for there was nothing they could do before daylight. The place was destroyed, the fire had already swallowed everything it wanted and had not made the jump from the clearing to the trees. The old woman had acted as if she hadn't heard him and just stood there with those damned spooky eyes of hers glowing. Miss McAdams couldn't convince the old lady either. Finally, in frustration, Martin snatched a kerosene lantern off the left side of the carriage and held it out to her.

"At least take this, ma'am," he said.

Instinctively, Miss McAdams reached out for the lantern but stopped herself when her eyes lighted on the glow of the flame inside. It was a look, not of fear—Martin doubted that this young woman feared anything—but some deeper angst. The driver himself balked at the look and began to withdraw the offer. Finally it was the old woman who stepped forward and grabbed the lantern from Martin's hand and then turned without a word.

Christ, he thought. What was a man supposed to do, and he yanked at the reins, turned the carriage round, and then whipped the horse violently into a gallop.

When Martin scrambled off the driver's seat at the front steps of The Breakers, the head liveryman was already up with his arms crossed and a stern look fixed on his face.

"Jesus glory, Tommy. Hold on, boy. You're going to shake that rig to pieces."

Martin pulled his hat off in deference to the livery man, who was considered a superior to all the valets and housemen and some say had been given the job by Flagler himself after serving the railway baron as a sort of sergeant-at-arms on his early trains into Florida.

"It's a fire, Mr. Carroll," Martin said, trying to control his voice. "In the Styx, sir."

Carroll turned his massive head to the south and then back on the young man before him.

"Were you not told that no one was allowed in the Styx tonight, Thomas?" Carroll said and the young man could not meet his eye.

"Yes, sir. But—"

"Then why the hell were you out there, son? And why aren't you over the bridge in town where you could be chasin' some local young lady at the fair instead of snootin' around in dark town?"

"I was taking Joe Shepard's late shift, sir. But—"

"But what? You lost a bet to Shepard in a dice game and now you're trying to add to your mark of stupidity?"

Young Martin was getting used to being ignored and berated this night and could not take his eyes off the toes of his boots.

"Don't worry about some fire in the Styx," the manager said, easing up on the boy. "It's none of your concern."

"But Mr. Carroll, sir. Miss McAdams and the old house woman, the one in charge of the maids. They're both out there, sir, and sent me for help."

The manager stared at the boy like he was trying to hear the statement with his eyes. Then he cursed once, spun on his heel and banged up the staircase. Before disappearing through the big front doors of the lobby he turned and ordered the young bellman to take the carriage to the livery "and cool that damned horse down before it catches a cold."

In the stables Martin shared the story with the livery watchman. Two Negro stable boys repairing harness in a back room overheard the words "Styx" and "fire" and one scrambled through the back stalls and headed on foot to the bridge to the mainland. And thus the news traveled in both directions, to the unofficial governors of Palm Beach and to the families who had paid a terrible price as they ate free ice cream and spun laughing and shrieking on carnival rides, oblivious of their fate.

CHAPTER THREE

Eɪɢʜᴛ ᴏ'ᴄʟᴏᴄᴋ ᴏɴ ᴀ Nᴏᴠᴇᴍʙᴇʀ ɴɪɢʜᴛ and the alcoholic braying of Jack Brennan was spraying out into the cold air of Manhattan's Lower East Side: "All hail Detective First Grade Michael Byrne on his bloody retirement from the New York City Pinkertons with all his teeth intact like the smile of a teenage whore whom we should all be so lucky as to meet tonight."

"Hooray!"

Byrne raised his pint, smiled his sheepish smile, which only exacerbated his old friend's ribald comments, and joined a half-dozen men in downing their ales in a long single draining. The end task was met by the slamming of glasses on the bar of McSorely's Pub, the shuffling of chair legs on raw wood floors and a call for another round. Byrne looked over the heads of the young men he'd helped train and then commanded. In the dull flickering light of McSorely's electric lamps they looked an almost civilized bunch. None of them over five foot eight, except for big Jack. None over a hundred and a half pounds. In the dimness you couldn't see the dirt at their neck collars or the worn seams of their waistcoats and trousers. But their hand-cropped haircuts were all the same, short and sharp. And without looking Byrne knew they all wore polished brogans on their feet, some of them for the first time in their lives wearing proper footwear. The shoes had been provided by the company, of course, and were the same style as those Byrne had on his own feet. The haircuts and boots were requirements of their employment with the Pinkerton security company they all worked for and set them apart from the street thugs and gang mobs. These were boys selected by the keen eyes of company scouts and their connections from the streets. They were a chosen few; perhaps selected because of a light of intelligence in their eyes, maybe because of a sharp, almost feral knack for survival through their wit, maybe because of a natural athleticism that set them apart in a fight. They were neighborhood kids like Byrne, rough-hewn from the tenements yet gilded with some touch of potential. Byrne had picked some of them himself, only a couple of years after he had been so singled out. An organization like the Pinkertons needed such young men—those with knowledge of the corners and garbage-strewn alleys of the city, those with an ear for the mixed languages of the streets where plans were set and crime was hatched.

Byrne reached down into the pocket of his trousers to feel the folded paper note once again, as he had dozens of times in the last several days. He wasn't sure why he carried it. He had already memorized the words in the telegram that Ian Cronin had passed him on the day of his mother's death:

mikey...it is time for you to join me...i will soon be taking a grand piece of property in Florida...i now have riches and land, what da always wanted...the rail tickets and money enclosed should get you and mother to west palm beach...i will meet you whenever you arrive...your big brother, Danny.

The telegram was the first time he'd heard from his brother in three years. Danny the first-born child. Danny the chosen one. Danny, supposedly the smartest of the boys and crowned as bearer of the family name. But after their father had died, Danny had turned sullen and angry and violent. His way of charming and schmoozing even the most cynical of the city dwellers of their last nickel or shoelace or pint had been his greatest talent. But you needed a pleasant twinkle and a bright patter and a patience to work such a magic, and Danny had lost all of that after seeing their father work his fingers stiff and his knees to creaking and his dreams to dust only to die in the muck and horse droppings of the street. One night after the old man's passing, Michael came awake in their bed and in the grey darkness he'd watched Danny move about the apartment, dressing and gathering his things. He watched his brother move like a shadow and bend and kiss their mother's quiet cheek. He'd squeezed his own eyes tight when his brother came back to their shared mattress and touched Michael's foot in a gesture of good-bye. He reopened his eyes in time to see Danny go to his parent' dresser and take their father's gold fob watch—the precious one with the blue steel hands and his initials scrolled on the back—from the top drawer.

It was not a theft. The watch had been willed to Danny and was his right. The last Michael saw of his brother was a final peeking eye when he carefully closed the door behind him as he'd often done when escaping into the night, but this time he'd gone and never returned.

The thoughts came again as Byrne touched the edges of the folded telegram in his pocket, rubbing the now soft edges with his fingertips. The tickets and money Danny referred to of course never made it to Michael. The telegram had been originally sent to his old New York Police Department substation. From there it had gone to a former sergeant who passed it on to Ian Cronin. Michael had not opened it until after his mother's burial, when he was back and alone in the empty walkup. He'd read in on the edge of the bed and carefully folded it and put it back in his pocket and there it burned, stirring his anger at the brother who'd abandoned him, swelling his resentment for being left to care for their mother alone. He'd given up on Danny's return and damned his brother's memory when he came creeping into his dreams at night. So why was he still carrying it? Why had he been so eager to jump at the offer to work a train going south in the morning? To see if it were true, this promise of land and money? Or maybe to ring his brother's neck if he could catch up to him? He'd gone to the telegraph office in midtown and asked the clerk to reply to the origin of the telegram:

Danny...coming to meet you...ma is dead...mike

Byrne questioned the terseness of the message now, the bluntness of it. But tough shit. Danny had tossed enough hurt at his family to deserve a bit of it back. He'd kick his brother's ass when he found him, he swore he would.

"Aye, Michael, here's to your bloody retirement," came another booming voice from yet another corner of the pub, and Jack Brennan again swaggered over and lifted his glass. "To the sharpest and the most civil among us lads," he hollered and tilted his head to Byrne. "And the most dangerous and merciless with his whip of steel."

Byrne raised his beer with the rest and smiled his smile and nodded his thanks and never said a word to anyone of his brother's telegram. To them Byrne was retiring, nothing more. Leaving New York would seem like falling off the edge of the world to the men. Just the thought of such a move would set them bragging about their wretched lives to whatever extent needed to cover their fear of leaving the Bowery, or Alphabet City or the Gas House District. None of them had ever stepped foot out of the neighborhoods. Yes, Byrne's sought-out reassignment would seem a retirement to them, and in a way he used the same term to try to fool himself and justify his mission. He'd become the old man of Pinkerton squad number eighteen, he'd say. At his age he was over the hill. It was time to let the younger bulls begin their rule, except of course at the top of the company where the big-bellied commanders and sharp-faced businessmen ruled the overall. But those heights were no place for a neighborhood kid like Byrne to climb, nor did he personally care to try. Tomorrow he'd take his newly acquired rank of detective and report for duty on a new railway line built by Henry Flagler, the oil magnate whose Manhattan mansion had been guarded by the Pinkertons for years. Tomorrow he would be headed toward a great unknown called the state of Florida.

But tonight Michael Byrne was here at McSorely's working his way toward alcoholic oblivion when a sudden rush of cold air from the front door of the tavern blew through and an immediate wave of commotion was started by an ungainly local urchin named Screechy.

Everyone knew the lad from the unhealthy look of his dull, copper-tinged hair and the high, raspy sound of his voice. The hair was discolored from a lack of nutrition and the voice had developed from an infancy of wailing for a mother who never responded. The combination should have killed the child before he was a toddler, but some impossible gift for self-preservation had saved him for the streets.

"Come on, then, Michael," big Jack yelped into Byrne's ear while grabbing him by the coat sleeve. "Screechy says the Five Points boys are havin' it out with the Alphabet City Gang over in Tompkins Square Park."

Screechy. Every time Byrne saw the kid he thought of Danny, the same feral nosiness, the same lust for everything in the streets and how it worked, especially the ways of the cons, the hooks, the pickpockets and hustlers. Screechy was Danny fifteen years ago, and like Danny, he had the ability to pull you into a place you shouldn't be going.

Most of Byrne's troupe was already started out the door, reinforced by their drunken buzz, following after the smell of adrenaline and violence. When Byrne hesitated, his old friend gave him that practiced look of impish amusement. "Just for a look-see, eh? Not that we have to get into it, you know?"

Out in the street the cold hit them all in the face. It had been near fifty degrees inside McSorely's, the place being heated by a single fireplace and the body temperature of a couple dozen men, but out here the temperature was below freezing and the lot of them thrust their hands into pockets and moved more or less as a group down Seventh Street east toward the park. By the time they'd reached Second Avenue and passed under the El the frosty air had sobered Byrne enough to start him second-guessing his decision to come along. In the light of the dim electric lamps on the avenue he could see the plume of his own breath and feel the hairs inside his nose crinkle with cold.

"What the hell, Brennan," he said, "has happened to my going away party?"

Half said in jest, the comment seemed to float in the darkness over his big friend's head as they made their way down the next block. Brennan's nose was up in the air as if sniffing at a trail to a feast. The big man stayed quiet, matching the quick steps of their group ahead until they crossed First Avenue and heard a human howling in the distance. From his higher vantage point, Brennan spotted torch flames in the distance.

"Your party has just become a bit more interesting," Brennan said, turning to his commander with a glint of excitement in the widening whites of his eyes. At that the lot of them broke into a jog, their matching brogans slapping the uneven cobblestone of the streets and heading for the edge of Tompkins Square.

At the first cry of impending violence, they stopped. Despite the efforts of the city when they revamped Tompkins Square Park to bring an open space to the jumbled stacks of tenements and street markets of the Lower East Side, the place at night was nearly as dark and shadowed as the alleyways around it. The new electric lights at all four corners did little more than add a luciferian flicker to the winter-bared trees inside the square. Some of the men went to their haunches, a tactic Byrne himself had taught them. Still, he and big Jack remained upright, using the night sight they'd gained from their childhoods on these streets to make an assessment.

"There, on the left," Jack said, his finger pointing to the north side of the park where they could now make out the flame of a torch.

"Aye and there on the South side," Byrne said, pointing out the torchbearer on the opposite side.

With that little light as a backdrop they could see the outlines of bobbing heads but the number was impossible to count. They could also make out the occasional flash of metal, maybe a pipe, maybe a long blade.

"Could be a dozen a side, maybe more," Jack said. "Five Points boys to the south."

Brennan could hear the disgust in his friend's voice. The Five Points Gang had been growing in viciousness and number since both of them were kids. If Brennan and Byrne had not been saved off the streets by a well-meaning New York City cop, they would have been sucked into the gang life just like the others they grew up with in the Gas House District. And the Five Points would be their natural enemy.

But from here they stood back and watched the dark gap between the torch flames begin to close, step by step, the silence of night now starting to fill with the shouts and curses of gang members stoking for the fight. When they heard the first guttural thump of flesh against flesh, all of Byrne's crew came to their feet, squinting into the dark to their right. Byrne knew the tactics of the Five Pointers. They would have sent some of their gang out to either side of the park's edge to flank the Alphabet City boys.

"Aye, ya little bastard," came a shout followed by the rustling of fast feet in the dry winter leaves. The Pinkertons now stood tall and almost instinctively closed ranks, shoulder to shoulder as the sound came closer. Then as if from behind a black tree came the rolling form of a small human being, spinning, head over hips and then gaining its feet for only a second before the man chasing behind sent a boot crashing against the boy and knocking him again to the ground.

"Ya shite! You warned 'em ahead of time didn't ya, ya little prick?" the big man yelled, re-cocked his leg and sent another toe into the boy's ribs. The muted squeal of pain came out from between the child's teeth, and from ten yards away Byrne recognized the tousled mop of reddish hair. "Screechy," he called out once before bounding up over the curb and into the park.

The Five Pointer's leg was again at the ready and the boy had curled to a ball, his elbows over his ears to protect his head, when the whipping sound of thin metal swept through the cold air and a shaft caught the gang member on the outside tendon of his support leg and dropped him like a sack of grain.

"Christ, Screechy, you should know how the hell to keep out of the big boys' brawls by now," Byrne said, standing over the both of them now with a metal baton in his hand that he'd pulled from his waistcoat. The boy peeked up at Byrne between skinny forearms and a smile started to come to his eye but quickly changed when they both heard the rustle of leaves. The Pinkerton detective's baton was still pointing down when a fist crashed against his temple.

Byrne rolled away at the last second and the punch caught him but had lost most of its force. The quick move also caused his attacker's weight to carry him past and Byrne used his pivot to bring the baton across the back of the man's head. He went face first into the dirt. But a companion was on Byrne immediately. Reinforcements had followed, but so too had Byrne's Pinkertons and the row was on.

He woke, as usual, freezing his ass off and dreading the darkness that would surely greet him as soon as he could pry his crusted eyes open. Byrne pulled the blanket tighter, curled his shoulders in and felt the pull of his clothes against the bed linens. He found the strength to move his feet and was relieved to find that he had at least taken off his brogans before climbing into bed. Yet, he still winced at the thought of putting his feet to wooden floors that were chilled like pond ice and then slipping his feet into frozen shoes. Which then, he thought, was going to be warming which?

He finally gained the willpower to force open his right eyelid and spied the dull light seeping through the northern window of the room. But when he squinted, he felt the small crackle and pull of blood-caked skin at the side of his face and quickly recalled the slam of a fist against his temple last night, his own retaliatory swing of his baton and the blur of adrenaline and the scrape and shove and wrestle of bodies and shouts and whistles of a familiar chaos.

Christ! He let his fingers come out from under the blanket and immediately probed around inside his lips, touching and counting his teeth, feeling for unnatural gaps and then recalling big Jack's toast to his smile, before the row, before he and his boys had left most of the Five Points flank men lying in the rotting leaves moaning from the precise whippings from their batons. None of his own men had suffered more than minor bruises, and to avoid any more confrontation, they'd grabbed Screechy by the scruff of the neck and hauled him back to McSorely's and forced him to drink a pint of lager and ordered several more rounds for themselves.

"Aye, Michael," Brennan had said. "My forewarnin' to anyone worth a listen about that steel whip of yours shoulda reached that Five Pointer puttin' the boot to young Screechy." Brennan had leaned in conspiratorially. "And I swear I heard Danny's voice comin' out of your own mouth when you sent the boy packin'. Just like your old brother done to you when you were just a straggler on the gang fights."

Byrne had tipped his last mug to mark the memory then barely recalled making his way in the dark with Brennan to his tenement south of Hamilton Fish Park. There was a blurred recollection of hugging his mate in a farewell while the both of them stood staring at the lights strung above the newly finished structure of the Williamsburg Bridge.

"You get out, you lucky bastard. Get out of this city before the bloody rats eat us all," Jack Brennan had said. "Go on to Florida, wherever the hell that is, and make a life for yerself away from this place."

Now it was his day of leaving. Yet he did not bolt from bed. He had plenty of time. Late morning train out. He lay still instead, watching his own breath stream out in jets of white into the single room. He did not move his head, putting off what he knew would be some pain from the fracas of last evening.

He shifted his slowly improving eyesight to the door opposite. The locks were set. Maybe he had not been as drunk as his pasty mouth indicated.

He lay there several minutes, planning what he'd have to pack—a few articles of clothing that he'd splurged on by having the washerwoman downstairs clean and hang out to dry. He stared at the old dresser drawer where a small leatherette held several keepsakes, including the papers his parents had kept and their documents from Ellis Island, their photographs blurred to sepia with age. And once it held his father's watch. The sight of Danny slipping it out of the drawer the night he left came into Byrne's head again. When their father died—their mother told them he'd been crushed under the wheels of a delivery wagon on his way to his job as an apprentice steamfitter—Michael had known that she'd lied. He was convinced that his father was alive because he knew the old man never went anywhere without the Swiss-made watch that he'd brought with him from Dublin and rarely let out of his sight.

Byrne shifted his eyes again, looked up to the single eastside window in the room and tried to will the light of a late sunrise in through its dirty panes. He thought of how proud his father had been to move them into this, the second floor of a building where they'd started out in the rat-infested basement, then to the top where the rickety stairs and lack of heat was the next stop for the poorest. Year by year his father had muscled and scrapped and used that optimistic smile of his to make friends, find connections, and get into a better job. The steamfitter job was one he'd been vying for, one to pay the forty-eight dollars a month they'd need to rent a flat farther north in a better neighborhood. But after two years there, the old man had started to change. The smiling eyes began to go dull at dinner. The full-throated Irish brogue that told wonderful stories at night went hollow and finally quiet. One night, Michael had risen from his cot to use the tenement's hallway bathroom and saw his father sitting up, staring out the only window of the apartment at a view that only contained the brick wall of the building across the street. His parents never argued those last two years. No complaints from his mother. No recriminations from his father. Then the man who'd broken his back, and perhaps his soul, to raise them, was gone.

Byrne could see the vision of his father that he'd formed in his own head afterward, the one of his sinewy, 140-pound body lying in the middle of the filthy street, the indentations of horse hooves carved into his skin, his legs twisted at impossible angles. But in the vision, now a million sleepless nights perfected in his mind, Michael never saw a mark on his father's face, never a change in his absorbed and intelligent eyes.

Of course, Michael had never really seen the body, had in fact never been to a funeral ceremony or a gravesite. All he and Danny were left with was the watch, the only thing of value their father had brought on the "Coffin Ship" from Dublin, with its plain ivory face and oval halo of silver. And that's how he knew his mother had lied.

Byrne gathered himself—he hated the cold—and then flung back the blanket and stood. The cold wood floor stung as he knew it would. He'd gone to sleep last night with his pants on and they would have to do for his journey. To his surprise he found that he'd actually taken off his shirt and hung it on the bureau. But when he held the bone-white garment up he could see even in the bare light that there were blood stains at the left shoulder, and that wouldn't do. He reached into his pocket, came out with a stick match, and lit the kerosene lamp on the bureau top. The flame crawled up the mirror before him.

The reflection was of a man with dirty-green eyes and high cheek bones. The aquiline nose was slightly bent, broken only once by a beer bottle, and the ears were somewhat large but pinned back as if in perpetual full charge. There was a dark streak running down the left side of the muscled cables of the neck, which appeared to start somewhere inside the light brown hair. He followed the trail up to a slick, sticky mass just above the ear. He touched the spot with his fingertips and could feel the sharp flash of open nerve endings but did not flinch. Byrne had always had an unnatural threshold for pain. He probed around the area a bit before determining the wound was minor and then went to the large metal sink that had been installed only a year ago when plumbing came to the building. He'd run a basin full of water and set it inside yesterday, not trusting that the pipes bringing water to the second floor would not be frozen in the early morning. Indeed, he now had to crush the top skin of thin ice on the porcelain, and then he dipped a rag and began cleaning the rip in his scalp that had likely come from a ringed fist or some lucky swat of a length of pipe during the fight last night.

He gathered the rag and the basin, moved to the bureau top and began washing his face with the now blood-tinged water. The crusted scrape on his left cheek came clean though raw, and the grime of soot, constantly in the city's polluted air, wiped off as well. He found both a bar of lather soap and a small bristle brush and lathered up his slight whiskers. He then bent to retrieve the single-bladed knife he always carried in a sheath strapped to his ankle. The instrument was small enough for concealment and had many uses, some routine, some that just happened to come along. He shaved himself clean. He would be meeting his new bosses today. Better to present his best. When he'd finished, he cleaned the blade and put it back in its holster and then packed everything he owned into a single old leather satchel. The fact that he had so little made no impression because no one he knew had much more. He donned the warm coat given to him by the same Pinkerton supplier who gave them all their shoes, took one last look around the apartment, to absorb its memories and its lessons, and locked the door behind him. The landlady would know soon enough when the rent was due that he had gone.

Outside, an early morning gloom was on the day, though it was always hard to tell whether it was the cloud cover or the density of coal smokeand ash hanging in the air. When Byrne stepped off the threshold he nearly bumped into old Mrs. McReady, who was mumbling and moving her equally old produce cart into position for the day. The woman was bundled in layers of dull and worn clothing that as far as Byrne could tell never varied, whether worn in the heat of summer or the freezing nip of winter. He had known the woman all his life and long before she'd lost her mind.

"Pardon, Mrs. McReady. Didn't mean to startle you," Byrne said, using a touch of the old country in his voice for her, a holdover that he tried to avoid when speaking to anyone else in the city who might take a dislike to him because of his heritage.

The woman looked up into his face with milky eyes and an illusory recognition.

"Danny, me boy. Good mornin' yourself and how is it you're so late gettin off to school?" she said, mistaking him for his brother as she always did and chastising him though he had not been school aged for a good ten years.

"No school today, Mrs. McReady, and it's me, Michael."

The old woman huffed at the correction, whiffed her hands and turned to wrestle with the handles of her cart, the diameter of the wooden posts thicker than her own tired legs. Byrne swung his satchel over his shoulder and helped her move the cart to the position where it had sat every day for two decades.

"Bless you, Mikey, but don't touch my cart again boy or I'll tell your mum and she'll whip you solid," the old woman snapped. Byrne would have laughed at the threat but for the image of his mother that instantly jumped into his head. She had never touched him in anger, and in her last years she'd barely had the strength to stand.

"I'd appreciate you not telling her, ma'am," he said to Mrs. McReady.

"Aye, this one time, boy." She reached in under the canvas that covered her cart and withdrew a small green apple and pressed it into his palm. "Now get on with you, you'll be late for school."

Byrne hugged the old woman, squeezing the rumpled bundle hard but was still unable to feel the bones hidden somewhere inside that magically kept her upright.

"So I'm off," he said as she stood there, her eyes gone vacant, looking befuddled and slightly stunned by the odd recognition of a man's arms around her if only for a second.

Byrne started north on Pitt, the sky in the east showing just a smoldering of light as if the sun was being held down by some giant gray fabric. The air was moist and the cold penetrating, the only advantage of winter was that the garbage and sewage in the streets was frozen, which kept the stench at a minimum. Though the streets were still empty of people, Byrne walked along the edges of buildings, head down and eyes up. By habit he knew that in these neighborhoods you did not draw attention to yourself regardless of your errand. As he skirted the western edge of Hamilton Fish Park he could make out the huge arch of the gymnasium, the place where New York Police Captain John Sweeney had found him and big Jack and others when they were boys and drafted them into a yet unofficial junior police crew. It was in that gym that Byrne had learned the use of the telescoping baton. Captain Sweeney had given him rudimentary anatomy lessons, nerve points on the human body, weak spots where grown men could be struck and quickly rendered harmless. That knowledge and his own mechanical perfection of the balance and design of the steel baton had impressed Sweeney and had saved Byrne's ass more than a few times on the streets.

When he and Jack Brennan were seventeen, Sweeney pulled them aside and told them he could pave their way into the city's police department. The pay would be minimal, but they'd have a chance at regular jobs, a perk that few like them could get without being beholden to the neighborhood bosses.

"You're smart boys. You know the streets and the characters out there. We need young men like yourselves to tap into what's going on so we can clean out some of the vermin, you know."

When Byrne took the offer to his brother, Danny scoffed in his face.

"I'll make more money in a week on Broadway than you will in a year," he said and Michael knew it was true. By then Danny was working as a barker out in front of the follies and running a gambling table in the basement of the place at night. Since they were kids Michael had tagged along but only watched, careful to stay out of slapping range of his brother's hand, but soaking up the atmosphere, the gestures, and the faces of pimps and prostitutes, opium sellers and dice shooters. He could still recall the day Danny was up on his soapbox while Michael sat on his heels in a nearby alcove. In his memory, he was filing away the details, the way his brother used his arms and hands to articulate his pitch, the voice he used, so different than his normal conversational voice, the eye contact, picking through the potential buyers versus those too smart or to conservative to take a chance. He memorized what clothes Danny wore, gaudy jackets and vests Michael had never seen at home that were either borrowed from other barkers or kept somewhere secret so their parents wouldn't know. But when Michael's eyes got to his brother's feet he noted that he was wearing mismatched socks—one checkered and one blue—and when he looked down at his own feet, he was wearing the exact same pair—one checkered and one blue.

Somehow, seeing Danny up close shielded him of the allure of it all. Instead he watched and memorized faces, names, the knowing winks, and the strange vernacular of a dozen languages and accents.

He may have admired his brother's way of dealing with the streets, but when Michael and big Jack got the chance to join the police, they both got hired on the spot with Sweeney's recommendation. They did some minimal training and were sent out as fodder to manage the traffic on Broadway, dancing in between the horse wagons and push carts and the pedestrians moving to and from the elevated and plowing beneath the iron structures. After the day's street duty they'd be called in as muscle in the so-called vice sweeps of the west side of Manhattan in Hell's Kitchen or to quell skirmishes between their own Irish brothers and the Negros living nearby in the San Juan Hill section.

After three years Byrne knew he was not made for the job. He lacked the ruthlessness of his sergeants and shrank at the orders of the ward bosses who called for the outright beatings of citizens who Byrne could plainly see simply couldn't afford to live in the neighborhoods or were of the wrong ethnic persuasion to stay there. He was also too adept at recognizing the graft and payoffs being made to authorities on a regular basis, a detailed accounting of which he'd brought to upper command only to be told to put his sharp eyes and ears to better uses and keep his Irish yap shut.

It was Captain Sweeney who saved him yet again and got him assigned to a special unit that was assembled to provide security against looting during the massive reconstruction of the Grand Central Terminal on Forty-second Street. There Byrne's eye and ear for both graft and outright theft gained the attention of the private contractors who cared more about their money than the ethnicity or social standing of those ripping them off.

When the Pinkerton agency made inquiries about hiring him away from the police two years ago, Byrne didn't hesitate. Now, after receiving Danny's telegram, it was he who'd gone to the agency bosses to ask them if he could have a position on a security team for the railroads. They'd been surprisingly quick to assign him. He now had an eight o'clock appointment on board a southbound train to Washington D.C. and points beyond.

So it was that Michael Byrne, the last of a New York immigrant family, found himself walking across East Houston in the chill dawn, skirting around a short line of Colonel George Waring's sanitation wagons. There he slowed to watch a group of men in white uniforms who were armed with ropes and a jury-rigged slide as they loaded the half frozen carcass of a horse that had been left where it dropped by some unlucky freight man overnight. Normally the crew would be shoveling black snow, a mixture of ice and garbage and refuse that was piled alongside the street, which would then be dumped in the East River. A dead horse was an occasional break in the routine. Byrne passed quietly and made his way west on Houston. His plan was to slide along the northern edge of the Bowery—better to avoid any trouble with the gang boys there who no doubt wouldn't be awake and out of their dens as of yet, but why take the chance. In the now dull light he could see the raised rails of the El running above Second Avenue. He estimated he had four miles to negotiate to reach Grand Central, but turned up First Avenue anyway. He wanted to walk his city one final time.

Heading north, he lengthened his gait on the wide sidewalks, absorbing the signage of a hundred businesses as he passed: a cutter displayed a giant pair of scissors at Third Street; a sausage maker had a huge worst protruding from his first floor shop at Fourth. At St. Marks Place the family crest of the Medici family with its three gilt balls indicated a pawnbroker. Byrne stopped at the intersection and looked east, where he could now see the skeletal trees of Tompkins Square, and he touched the side of his face with his fingertips where the bruise from last night was still tender, but he smiled at the recollection of his wand against the back of the head of a Five Pointer.

The farther north he marched the better the business venues. Still, most of them had adopted an old world style of hanging their signs out over the sidewalks to gain attention: an enormous pair of eyeglasses advertised an optician; an outsized cutout of a violin for a musical instrument shop.

Soon he began to move through areas of a class where he rarely traveled unless on police business and where, as a citizen, he didn't belong. Large, multistoried homes of stately architecture adorned the side streets, although age and the city's constant soot and pollution had stained their facades. Even the rich could not partition off the air. Past Fourteenth Street, he glanced west and could see the buildings of Stuyvesant Square Park, named after one of the richest patriarchs of the city, where he had once delivered a man of means to the New York Infirmary after a beating in a brothel down on Bowery. It was all done quietly of course, but despite warnings from his superiors, Byrne had never forgotten the man's name and had tucked it away for some future use.

His ability to remember even the most mundane details was something Captain Sweeney had both praised Byrne for and warned him against.

"You've a sharp mind, lad. Wasted down here and truth be told, wasted in this department, considering. Mind that memory of yours doesn't get you in trouble, Michael. Some things are best forgotten in this godforsaken life. The reason you're here, hell, the reason we're all here is to forget the past and move on to a better future, boy. Don't let what's already happened get in the way of what can be."

Byrne had listened intently to the man's lessons. And as was his nature, he would never forget a single word, or anything else that cared to strike his mind.

Within another mile, he began to feel anxious, a shiver of nerves running into the muscles of his upper back. Ahead were the red brick walls of Bellevue Hospital, the notorious house of the mentally deranged. Byrne had not forgotten a single whispered word that he'd overheard between his mother and neighbors after his father's disappearance on a winter day years ago.

"Screechin' like a madman, he was, Ann Marie."

"Wild as a cut beast one minute, starin' inta the afterworld the next."

"It was in his eyes, luv. Ya can't deny that. His mind was gone."

"It's the best, Ann Marie. Before he turns on ye and the boys."

"Three times this month, Ann. Naked in the freezin' street. He's insane, woman. Deal with it."

His mother always denied it. She would never admit that she'd had their father, her own husband, committed. The tale told to her sons about their father's accident on the street had been her story and she stuck to it.

But after he'd been made a cop, Byrne would ask for his father by name at Bellevue and a dozen other madhouses in the city whenever he was in a district on assignment. He tried to make it sound official, as if he were investigating a crime. The intake officials would sometimes pretend to go through the lists, finally looking up to give him a raised eyebrow that only meant that for a bit of a bribe they might have someone who fit the description. He'd even paid a couple of times at first, only to have some poor bugger marched out who was a foot shorter or some dark-skinned European who would no more pass for Irish than an African slave. But even the old white-skinned wretches they'd bring forward, Byrne could always tell by the eyes. He would know his own father's eyes if he saw them again, even if they had gone insane.

Today he had to march on. Was he giving up the search for a father whom he still believed was lost if not dead? Yes, he supposed he was. He had someone else to search for now, and a train to Florida was a portal to that quest. As he walked north the smell of the East River blew in, an air salty and fresh mixed with the refuse and excrement piled along its banks. He took out his own cheap watch and checked the time: seven fifteen. The sidewalks around him were already starting to busy up with pedestrians, their nostrils blowing with steam as they made their way through still freezing temperatures. They were mostly laborers at this time of day, men in the trade uniforms of construction and iron workers and steamfitters moving west as he was now along Forty-second Street. Within two blocks he could see the enormous train shed of the new Grand Central Station rising up at Lexington Avenue. The glass and steel construction dwarfed everything around it, and it was not yet finished. Already Byrne could hear the clanging echoes of iron against iron, the dragging friction of hard stone being moved. He went through the instructions in his head: meet with Pinkerton detective Shawn Harris on lower track three aboard the southbound train to Washington D.C.

Byrne had worked the station as a cop, when it was in different stages of construction, but when he entered the enormous waiting area this morning and looked out from the staircase it was still bewildering in size and scope. Sixteen thousand square feet of chiseled and carved stone and marble, and across the way a cast-iron eagle with a wingspan that had to be the equal of any wagon on the street outside. Byrne stood a full five minutes, staring at the movement of people below, appearing in miniature like insects scurrying to assignments unknown. Unconsciously, he reached inside his coat and touched the shaft of his baton. He could not help but think of himself as like them, impotent BBs in a boxcar, as he moved down to join them.

At an information kiosk he was directed to the southbound Hudson River Railroad line below. In the bowels of the building the noise created by the massive steam engines and their giant wheels screeching along steel rails was an assault on the ears and caused Byrne to narrow his eyes in a grimace. Making his way in the directions given, he had to search through clouds of smoke and steam to find the numbered markers and letterings. He stopped a uniformed railway worker and shouted in his ear: "The Flagler departure?"

In response he got a finger wagged in a northerly direction, and of the response shouted back, the words "number ninety" was all he could make out. With his shoulders hunched as if to shield his chest from the onslaught, Byrne made his way down the platform, dodging the wheeled wooden carts of baggage handlers and the occasional geyser of steam spurting from the undercarriage of the train until his attention was snatched by a handsome forest-green rail-car with the gold gilded lettering "90" expressed on its façade. He took a step back to take in the entire car. Above the row of windows the name Florida East Coast Railway flickered in the same gold lettering. It was Flagler's private rail car. Since he couldn't determine by sight which end of the train car held the back door he approached the most northern end, putting one foot onto the iron stair step. When he stood up, his nose met the knee caps of a large man balefully staring down into his face.

"My name is Shawn Harris," the man said. "And you had best be one Michael Byrne, lad. Or your ass is mine."

After he had assured the estimable Mr. Harris that he was indeed Michael Byrne, he was allowed to board the train "after you wipe the grime and shite from those company shoes, m'boy. We don't allow that part of New York City to travel aboard Mr. Flagler's railroad."

Once his soles were passable, Byrne climbed up the wrought iron stair and joined Mr. Harris inside the car. The warmth was the first of several surprises Byrne encountered as the two men entered.

"This, lad, is number 90," Harris said with a sweep of his giant paw. The grand movement instantly struck Byrne as out of place for a big Irish thug of a former cop. But he soon understood the man's pride.

The interior walls of the Mr. Flagler's private car were paneled in a light-colored satin wood and framed in hand-carved white mahogany that even without the aid of the electric lamps gave the place a feel of sunshine that was the polar opposite of the dark, polluted gray of the city Byrne had just walked through.

Passing through the sitting areas and a desk surrounded by shelves of gilt-bound books, Byrne was aware that he'd unconsciously pulled in his elbows and turned his hips as not to come even close to touching anything. The furniture was upholstered in decorative floral designs of greens and gold, as were the carpeting and curtains. Harris looked back with a raised eyebrow and warning tip of his chin to the gleaming bronze chandelier as he maneuvered his big head around its cut glass. Byrne looked up, even though he knew his own height did not in danger of touching the object, but he noticed when he did that even the Empire ceilings of the car were put him and decorated with gold leaf. His mouth must have been hanging open, for Harris cleared his throat and winked at the younger man's show of amazement. As they passed through the dining area he saw the fireplace, flames dancing at a low level, which explained the warmth of the place. He'd barely had time to take in the opulence when Harris opened a door and they both stepped out onto the open balustrade at the opposite end of the car. The shot of cold in his nostrils caused Byrne's eyes to water, and Harris let him take a second to adjust.

"That, my young detective, is Mr. Flagler's sanctuary, and our number one duty is to keep out anyone that don't belong inside.

"Mr. or Mrs. Flagler or his chief, Mr. McAdams, are consulted directly before any person is allowed to enter. You screw that assignment up, lad, and you'll be off the train regardless of whether she's stopped or still movin', eh?"

"I understand, sir," Byrne said, giving the sergeant his due respect even though he was still measuring the man.

"Good," Harris said. "We run shifts on the fore and aft platforms when we're stopped for loading or unloading and especially when we spend anytime overnight on a side track for any reason.

"Mr. Flagler considers number 90 to be his hotel room on the road so that's the way we protect it and him."

Byrne nodded, absorbing as he always did, and then working out a response if indeed a response was even called for.

"Protect from who?" he finally figured it best to ask.

"Ha!" Harris gave a snort, which Byrne was soon to realize was his standard guffaw at all things he understood and felt others didn't. "From the same goddamn scalawags and supposed business moochers that you guard him from in the city, boy. 'Cept here they're more brazen cause maybe they think since they're on the same train as he is that he's like their neighbor or something. Most of these wags wouldn't dare walk up to the man's house or office in the city but think they can come right through the train cars to his door and tap him for an audience."

As a cop, Byrne had indeed once been ordered to provide "security" for the Flaglers' mansion on Forty-second street, just a few blocks west of Grand Central on a night when a crowd of so-called protesters had gotten their courage up to march against the rich and powerful. After a minor scuffle with a knot of the more drunk and aggressive of them, it had been one of the more boring nights he'd spent on the police force. Yet he knew even now that the small legend of that night had somehow led to this very day.

"Then there's the beggars and assorted nasties who try to push their way through when we're at some common rail stop along the way down south," Harris said. "But I don't figure that's going to be a problem for you, eh, Byrne."

And there it was. Proof of what wouldn't be said to him directly when his Pinkerton commander came and gave him this assignment.

Harris was giving him that wink and a grin that meant he wanted the story from the origin. Byrne pretended he didn't understand and simply nodded.

"Oh, come on lad. At least show me this little piece of weaponry I've heard bragged on by men I'd have to admit aren't easily impressed."

Byrne had already anticipated the inevitability of the request, and in a motion like a magician's flick of a satin scarf, the baton flashed up in his hand with a whisper and was instantly in front of his face, bringing Harris' eyes up to meet his.

"I heard there were six men, big men mind you, lyin' in the gutter outside Mr. Flagler's house within less than a one minute round," Harris said, focused on the short steel wand. "Boys said you never skinned a knuckle, never drew your gun."

"There were only four," Byrne said, and then with a snap of his forearm, the baton telescoped to three times its length with a sound like a switchblade being opened. "And they weren't that big."

The display did not make Harris jump, only his hand moved, tucking quickly into the thick breast flap of his coat.

"Aye," he said, now measuring the piece of steel from its tip to Byrne's fist and then looking back up to the younger man's eyes. "Let's get you back to the caboose, lad, where we'll have some breakfast and I'll fill you in on the rest of your duties before he himself gets here."

Byrne jumped down from the steps onto the platform, landing lightly on his toes. He could feel the big Irishman's eyes on the back of his shoulders and knew it was he who was now being measured. He retracted his baton and tucked it away in an inside pocket where it would be easily accessible.

CHAPTER FOUR

IT WAS BARELY EIGHT O'CLOCK AND the sun was already heating the back of Ida May Fluery's indigo blouse. She could feel internal heat rise to the collar at her throat and spread up to the perspiration beading on her wide dark forehead. She was standing on the very same spot where she had so often stood—at the head of the cul de sac in the Styx, organizing if she needed to, greeting when she wanted to, and cajoling when she had to. But this morning there was no shade on the hard-packed sand in front of what had been her home. The tree cover was now blackened and bare, the sun streaked through still rising wisps of brown smoke. This morning Miss Ida was giving out prayers and consolation in whispers and small tight hugs to the residents of her community.

Ida had not slept. She'd remained up throughout the night, helplessly watching until the flames that consumed every dwelling in the Styx had finally eaten all they could and then settled down as coals glowing like lumps of living, satisfied evil.

Last night when word jumped across the railroad bridge to West Palm Beach that the Styx was burning, a handful of her neighbors made it across the lake before some official closed off access to the island, stating that only firefighters were allowed across. No one, of course, of any such capacity ever arrived at the site of the blaze. Ida was there. So too were a couple of the stable boys and three cooks who were on duty at the Royal Poinciana Hotel on the lakefront a mile or so away. The boys had made foolish attempts to run in close to the flames to rescue things they deemed valuable. The women simply stood and watched and wept. By sunup an assistant hotel manager, a southern white man of indeterminate age, had arrived and gently herded the onlookers back to the Breakers with the promise of food and clean uniforms and then with equally gentle words reminded them that they still had to report for work today.

When the manager stood in front of Ida May she seemed to look straight through him.

"Mizz Ida," he said quietly, "ya'll going to have to supervise your people back at the hotel, ma'am."

Her eyes were not those of some unfortunate in shock, but of a woman who could envision her duties on some chalkboard slate only she could see.

"I will do my supervising from here, sir," she said, tempering her manner as not to sound like she was giving the orders. "May I suggest sir, that when folks are finally allowed to cross back from West Palm, you could please have a few at a time come out to their houses. I will make sure they can see what they need to see, sir. Then I'll get their work schedules right and send them back.

"Will that be acceptable, sir?"

The assistant manager seemed to focus on something slightly beyond the crown of her head while he considered how to explain it to his own superiors and make the plan his own.

"I'll take these folks with me," he said. "And send the next directly."

When he walked away Ida took up her spot in front of the ashes of her house and supervised the comings and goings. She watched the disbelieving expressions of each new arrival as they approached the blackened cluster of charred timbers and ash. And when the faces broke with despair or with anger, she passed her whispers of strength or possibilities along.

"Gone be alright now, Mazzie. You safe, that's all that matters. Right?"

"Careful now, Earl. You know the Lord don't take anything ya'll really need. You know that, Earl. Right?"

"It's OK now, Corrine. Come here, give a hug, sweetheart. Your children are all safe, right? They with you and that's everything, you know?"

After an hour or so that particular group would straggle back from their individual tragedies, their skin smeared with soot, the men carrying the head of some metal tool or heat-warped tin box, the women with a scrap of seared cloth, a blackened iron cook pot or an empty, charred picture frame.

Marjory McAdams was aboard the third wagonload to arrive. She had left the Styx while it was still dark and the sparks of the fire were just beginning to settle. She'd waited there with Ida May for hours after young Thorn Martin had left in the calash, promising he'd soon return with help.

"I cannot believe someone hasn't responded," she'd said in the middle of the night, looking expectantly back down the road to the hotel as if a fire brigade would surely come swinging round the corner at any second like it was midtown Manhattan. Ida May had ignored her comments, knowing the truth and thus the futility in the young woman's expectations. Marjory had finally given up trying to talk Ida into returning to the hotel with her and had marched off on foot. When she returned now, she had not changed her clothing, which was still soot-stained. Her face had been hastily wiped clean but she had not even taken the time to change her shoes, which were dust-covered, as was the bottom eight inches of her skirt. In the light of day, the destruction before her had changed from the smoky blur of varying shades of gray and black to the stark outlines of broken angles and spires of charred wood pointing oddly up like giant corroded fingers. The rising wind from the ocean had just begun to sweep the browned wisps of smoke from the surrounding treetops. Marjory waited until the new arrivals passed Miss Ida's consoling whispers and then watched them as they walked into the remains, their heads moving back and forth, taking in the alien sights and saying nothing. When they had all wandered off she approached the head housekeeper, softly cupped her shoulder and bent her cheek to the woman's grayed and soot-stained head.

"I have heard that everyone has been accounted for, Mizz Ida. Everyone is alive. Thank the Lord that the fair drew most everyone across the lake. That in itself is a blessing."

The old woman did not move her head, neither away from nor into the consoling hug of the young white girl. Her only reaction was a slight movement of her cheeks, which sucked in as if a small taste of bile had entered into her mouth.

"My father says Mr. Flagler is on his way from New York City this very day," Marjory said. "You know he'll take care of you all. He's a good man. My father said there is no doubt that he will find quarters for you either at the hotel or across the lake so don't you worry."

Ida did not respond. She had been across the lake many times to the new city of West Palm Beach. The cheap, tossed together buildings did not bother her. And the few merchants there were just starting out so they were not yet profitable enough to turn away colored folks with money to spend. Ida had even gone to a service there at the Tabernacle Missionary Baptist Church, which was a simple wood plank structure built on pilings on a plot of scrub pines at the edge of the town. She recalled the preacher as young and full of a heartfelt passion. So the idea of moving yet again was not something she feared. Ida had made new starts before. This would be no different than her family's move from Charlotte when the Abernathy family began buying up farm acreage to expand that city, or in Savannah years later when she'd been displaced by a new mercantile warehouse being built near the waterfront. As a woman whose family had always worked for others, Ida May Fluery knew the rules of the real world: when money comes to a place, those who are not owners are pushed aside.

Her natural skepticism, born of nearly sixty years of experience, told her this situation was no different. No different, that is, until screams started sounding from the far depths of the Styx.

The horses were the first to hear. The team had just started to pull away with a wagon load of residents when their ears pricked up at the unnatural sound, then their nostrils flared and they balked in their traces.

Miss Ida may have picked it up next and mistook the high, keening noise as some kind of animal cry. But the third wail, closing quickly from the east, caught the attention of everyone at the clearing and all of those in the wagon and they all turned their heads.

"What in Christ's name now?" said the driver.

In the distance the image of Shantice Carver could be seen stumbling into view, and Miss Ida let a snort escape through her nose. Marjory looked at her in surprise as she had never witnessed a derogatory utterance come from the woman in the two years she'd known her. The young Carver woman was in a half jog, her arms bent at the elbow and hands up in her face as if to cover her eyes from some horrific sight, yet her fingers were splayed enough to allow her to see where it was she was running to. With her arms in such a position, she seemed to toddle more than run and the high-pitched noise coming from her mouth gradually turned from unintelligible screeching to words: "Theysaman, theysaman, theysaman..."

No one moved to meet her, but the anguished cries seemed to pull Marjory out of her initial shock and she alone stepped forward. She realized the distraught figure was certainly more than a girl and from the bouncing of her bosom was more in the line of a young woman. Still, she took the poor thing by the shoulders and allowed her to bury her face into her own neck as if comforting a child.

"It's OK now, it's OK."

Despite the tableau of emotion, those in the wagon were now only mildly interested, as if they had seen such a display before, or had reason not to feel much compassion for this one of their own. But Miss Ida relented and walked over to the embrace between the two women, which had gone on long enough to have become an embarrassment.

"All right, Shantice. All right," Miss Ida said with a voice not exactly comforting but still understanding of the situation. "It's a hard time for everyone. What has you so all tore up, girl?"

At the sound of Ida's voice the woman stepped back away from Marjory and again her fingers went fluttering up into her face.

"Theysadedman, theysadedman, theys..."

"All right, all right, now slow down, woman. Cain't nobody understand what you're trying to say with all that screechin'. You take a good long breath now and slow down." It was obvious that the woman had taken stern orders from Miss Ida enough times in the past to nod her head and immediately start to suck air into her mouth and begin to swallow. Her next words were both several octaves lower and decibels quieter.

"Mizz Ida, ma'am. They is a dead man yonder near my place."

This time those listening in the wagon began to rise and jump down on the ground. The driver was now too entranced himself to complain though he stayed in his seat.

"All right. All right, Shantice," Ida repeated. She reached out to take the woman's shaky hands in her own and covered them as if calming both of their hearts.

"Who is it, Shantice? Tell me who it is that's dead?"

Now the small group was stone silent, waiting for grief to slap them.

"It's a stranger, ma'am," the woman called Shantice said. "I ain't never seen him before, ma'am, honest to God."

Ida's brow furrowed in skepticism, a reaction that caught Marjory by surprise as much as the woman's plea for believability.

"Now, Shantice, get yourself together, woman. You know every man in the Styx and most every other man on this here island. You think hard who you seen out there," Ida ordered the woman.

"I ain't never seen him, ma'am. God's truth. He's all burnt up, an he gots money..." At this point the woman's hands started back to fluttering and her voice began to cry and climb. "He gots money in his mout," she finally said, her fingertips now dancing near her own lips.

With the new information Ida shook her head with incredulity and started to turn back into the group as if this tale was a child's exaggeration that went beyond belief at a time already full of unbelievable events.

"An he's white, Mizz Ida," Shantice blurted out, her words catching the elderly woman in midstride and freezing everyone within hearing distance. "It's a dead white man."

CHAPTER FIVE

THE TRAIN WAS READY WHEN FLAGLER was ready.

After a breakfast of hot oatmeal and weak coffee, during which his new supervisor gave him his duties until such time they were out of the city, Michael Byrne was positioned at the head of Flagler's car number 90 where he was instructed to "stand ready like a Pinkerton man and don't let anyone approach while Flagler and his wife are boarding."

With a newly requisitioned knee-length woolen coat, Byrne stood rather comfortable in the cold, his hands clasped behind his back like he'd been taught as a police recruit, only moving up and down the loading platform. No one was within a car's length of number 90. The other passengers and material being loaded were up the tracks where the less glorious coaches and boxcars were aligned.

Byrne cut his eyes to the north when a contingent finally arrived out of the clouds of steam. Flagler was not difficult to pick out. He was the one in the middle, wearing a dark suit without an overcoat despite the cold. He was of average build—about five-foot seven and a thin one hundred and forty—despite his reputation as a giant of the business world. His most distinguishing feature was his full head of snow-white hair and a thick broom mustache to match. His back was straight, his chin held high, and his gait was best described as leisurely. He moved at a slow pace, though not because of any obvious infirmity. He was simply not a man in a hurry, nor one who needed to be.

Byrne knew little about the man other than he was rumored to be in his late seventies and had long ago become rich as the partner of John D. Rockefeller when the two of them established the Standard Oil Company. His was a station of the upper class that a man like Byrne was well to stand out of the way of and at attention to. Flagler's world was nothing that a working-class Mick such as he could ever understand, nor would he want to. They're different, the rich, and so be it.

Walking a half-step behind Flagler was a woman whom Byrne assumed was his wife. He was careful to only glance at her as not to catch her eye, and he noted that just from her profile she looked many years younger than Flagler and was dressed in the fine conservative style of a woman of means. Her skirts were not flowing; her coat was not of ostentatious fur or fabric. Her dark hat was certainly large but plumed with only a small shaft of feathers the kind Byrne had never seen even though he'd stood guard at several dignitary functions or special performances at the Metropolitan Opera.

Following behind the couple was Flagler's personal valet and a phalanx of business types carrying briefcases. And then the porters wheeling an entire baggage cart loaded with luggage. Harris nodded an unspoken greeting to Flagler and then helped Mrs. Flagler with a hand boarding the step rail. Then the two disappeared into their car. Byrne would barely see even a glimpse of them for the rest of the trip.

He and Harris helped load the baggage, and within ten minutes of Flagler's arrival, the train whistle ripped through the enclosed space under Grand Central Station and the train pulled out.

Hours later Byrne's eyes were still watering, and it was from something besides the cold. The train was only minutes out of the rail yards at Jersey City, heading south. There was something foreign in the air that seemed to sear the insides of his lungs when he took deep breaths. He was stationed at a designated spot at the forward door to private car number 90, where Harris had placed him.

"No one goes past you without Mr. Flagler's personal word," Harris had instructed. "I'll be back once we get underway again and take you on a bit of a tour."

So Byrne stood on the outside platform and found that if he inched his back close to the adjoining car in front, he was able to withstand the cold by hunkering down into the turned up cowl of the coat and burrowing his hands deep in its pockets. The morning's events—seeing Flagler and his entourage close up, the glimpse of the rich interior of the private train car that he was to guard and the melancholy sight of New York City fading behind them—had spun so quickly in his head he was just now able to use the minutes alone on the platform to assess his decision to take on this assignment.

If he was to be nothing more than a bodyguard for Flagler and a watchman for his rail car then he'd made a mistake. The work that he'd done for Captain Sweeney—putting together the names of certain Tammany bosses and politicians and documenting their travels to and from the opium dens and brothels of the Lower East Side—had come with the promise of a certain career. Sweeney had been impressed by young Byrne's ability to write, a skill not learned through schooling but from pure memory and copying of words and phrases picked up from newspapers and signage on the streets and the handbills that Danny was sometimes paid to give out. Sweeney had then been shocked further by Byrne's photographic memory of faces and seemingly flawless ability to attach names to such faces.

The young police officer's lists and detailed observations had, according to Sweeney, been invaluable in the department's battle against corruption, but the changes would be slow in coming. At one point, the captain had said it was too dangerous for Byrne to stay in the department. Thus, the Pinkerton offer.

The arrival of Danny's telegram had been an additional push and had given him this Florida destination and Sweeney encouraged it.

"A perfect solution. Go south into the sun for awhile, Michael," Sweeney said. "It'll be like a fine vacation and then you can come back home when things calm down a bit and these bastards from Tammany Hall are out on their arses. Then we've got a job waiting for you, son."

But now he was second-guessing, watching the buildings of Jersey City shrink down with each mile and the landscape becoming greener and more expansive than he'd ever witnessed as a city boy. Florida seemed a foolish dream now. What if he couldn't find his brother? What the hell would he do in the sun anyway? Only rich New Yorkers or people with tuberculosis went to Florida seeking a place to stay warm and breathe more easily. As if the thought alone caused it, Byrne bent over in a coughing fit, and as if on cue Harris nearly knocked him overboard coming through the door to the other cars.

"Don't be afraid of it, lad," Harris said, again sporting the smile that said, I know what you don't know. "It's the air, son. Your city lungs'll have to get used to it."

Byrne straightened and spat down onto the rail bed rushing by below.

"Why," he said, wiping his mouth with the back of his sleeve. "What's in the air?"

"Nothing," Harris said, now starting to laugh. "There's nothing in it but clear, clean air the likes of which you haven't taken a breath of since you were born in some Irish tenement what with the soot and smoke and rubbish stink of place.

"It's like a taste of pure water that you pour into your mouth for the first time. It's so different your body isn't ready for it. Keep breathin', boy. It's good for you."

Byrne took a shorter breath, but his eyes were on Harris, and the burn of his deprecating tone was running up into his ears.

"Your name isn't Harris is it?" he finally said, his eyes holding the big man's.

The older detective lost his smile.

"It was O'Hara when my father and two sisters got to New York in 1860, lad. The old man figured it was better changed unless you wanted to starve with the rest of the Irish. You might do well to consider it, Byrne," Harris said. "Now, let's take a walk."

Harris led the way, passing slowly through the first passenger car, touching the top corners of each seat as he passed. The gesture was made not to collect his balance—his experience of walking through the rolling train was like that of a seaman and he rarely wavered—but to signify some sense of ownership to the riders he seemed to study one at a time.

Byrne followed, but his sea legs were not yet established. He pitched side to side with the sway of the cars and twice bumped into the shoulders of men sitting on the edge of the isle.

"Pardon me," he said both times.

When they left the first car and stood on the outside connecting platform, Harris lectured him.

"Don't ever offer apologies, lad. You're security here and the likes of them know that just from the look of you." Harris tipped his chin back toward the car. "A little respect goes a long way if somethin' should occur. It also warns 'em if they start to think they can cross you. You know what the uniform does on the street? It's the same here. You want them to know you're Pinkerton."

Byrne knew the tactic: force and bully. It was not a method he preferred. His best work was done undercover, working the sidelines and shadows. He did not fear direct confrontation, the steel whip in his hand was more than effective, but he liked the advantage of observing trouble first before jumping into it.

"Now let's see that talent of yours that Captain Sweeney bragged on to get you there," Harris said. "I'll go through the next car. You follow in five minutes and I'll meet you on the next platform."

Byrne waited until the door closed on Harris' back and then slipped his watch from his pocket, checked the time. Out in the midmorning sun he watched as the landscape changed to bare winter trees and chilled brown shrubbery and the occasional rail siding flashing by. He closed his eyes and took a deep breath of the air and this time he held it without choking. The smell was of leaves decomposing on the ground, not unpleasant like the odor of rot, but something simply changing and refueling the soil. It was a sensation completely foreign to him.

When the five minutes had passed Byrne opened the door to the passenger car and walked through at a pace that was unhurried, but not so slow as to draw attention. No one fails to at least look up as a stranger passes by in such close quarters, but what they notice, and what each one remembers, is the key. Captain Sweeney had obviously passed on word of Byrne's ability.

When he stepped out onto the open platform, Harris was waiting with a smarmy grin on his face, arms folded across his broad chest almost in the manner of a challenge.

"OK, lad. Tell me what you saw."

"Twelve passengers," Byrne started, "Seven men and two women in their midtwenties. The women are both married. Three children, two of them girls. The younger of the women with her son is nervous enough to be holding her St. Christopher's in her left hand. Her shoes are the kind a woman who had several miles and days to go would wear. The other woman is wary of men. She keeps cutting her eyes up at the old guy up front and flinched hard when I came even with her shoulders. Her clothes make her a social elite. If she's going to Philadelphia, her husband is probably a businessman."

Harris had stopped grinning and stared at Byrne's eyes.

"And the gentlemen?"

"Not a farmer among them," Byrne started. "The three by themselves are salesmen is my guess by the worn threads on their jacket cuffs and the resoled shoes. The valises they have are probably filled with samples and clean white shirts.

"The three fellows facing each other in the middle are interesting. They're playing three-card Monte, but there's no money being exchanged. It looks like the two on the north seats are actually teaching the scam to the other. By his accent, he's probably a Pole from Brooklyn. I'm not sure about the document briefcases they all seem to be carrying. But shysters sometimes all look alike even when they aren't trying."

By now Harris had raised that spiked eyebrow of his and had dropped his folded arms to rest on his newly relaxed belly.

"And the last?" he said.

"Older man." Byrne hesitated before picking his words. "A poor man's version of Mr. Flagler himself. The cigar wallet in his suit coat pocket. Three rings, one with a nice stone. The shoes are new and expensive, but the collar of his shirt is too off-white for professional laundry. That briefcase he's got next to him has a lock on it, never seen one of them before."

Again he hesitated.

"Is that all?" Harris said.

"The old guy was studying me as much as I was him. Nothing gets past that one. Reminds me of Sweeny himself."

"Aye," Harris said. "And the old captain didn't let you slip past either, did he now. Right as rain he was with the likes of you, young Byrne. Talent as advertised. Now I'll have to worry about you takin' my own job."

Byrne did not blush at the compliment. He'd been asked to demonstrate his photographic memory before and he had not shown Harris even the beginning of his abilities.

He was later to learn that the women were indeed wives, one of a Philadelphia investment banker and the other meeting her husband who was homesteading a piece of land in Florida. She would continue with them for the entirety of the trip. The salesmen were just that, men working the connections between New York and Philadelphia. The three budding card sharks were "binder boys," as Harris called them. They were young men who'd put chunks of money together through whatever means: beg, borrow or steal. Now they were headed for Florida and the promised land of booming real estate. Harris again explained that these three would join a growing number of speculators who had found early on that previously useless land in the newly blossoming cities along Mr. Flagler's rail line was gaining in value by the day.

"The crooks'll get a stake from some business type in New York and come down and buy a binder on the sale of a piece of land and then slap away the mosquitoes while the price keeps risin'," Harris said.

Harris explained that a binder was a nonrefundable down payment that required the remainder of the cost of the land to be paid within thirty days.

"They might swat the insects for twenty days, maybe even twenty-eight before they sell it again before the final payment is due. And the profit, m'boy. You ain't never seen the price of land climb the way it does in Florida.

"I watched a binder pass through six hands before the last fool got caught holdin' the bag with no more buyers around. But hell, this is just the beginning of these rascals. That group is goin' to the end of the line in Miami, and believe me, they're playin' three-card Monte with land deeds down there, lad."

Byrne filed the information away. It takes money to make money, unless of course you're a thief or taking advantage of someone else's cash. Those weren't hard lessons to learn on the streets of the Lower East Side. They were also lessons he'd watched his brother Danny employ on a regular basis. If there were three of a kind in the business of fleecing someone, maybe they had run across Danny in their travels. He'd find an acceptable time and place to speak again with that group.

"And what about the gentleman?" Byrne said, wanting the same background on the older man who had eyeballed him.

Harris tried to straighten his face to give a flat look that was a mighty effort for a rough Irishman.

"Faustus," he said. "Stay clear, Byrne. He'll be tryin' to recruit you to some unholy religion that'll lead to trouble that we have no part of and no relation to. Leave that sleepin' dog lie, hear?"

Byrne was ordered to again take up his post on Mr. Flagler's car while they made a short stop at the North Philadelphia station where the Germantown and Chestnut Hill lines merged. Soon enough they crossed the deep running Schuylkill River and merged onto yet another line. Byrne watched the landscape change yet again as they approached the city and caught sight of charred destruction. It became evident that the main rail station had recently been destroyed by fire, and although the tracks had been cleared, there was still the scent of charred and smoldering wood in the air. Byrne coughed and thought of his new sensitivity to clean air and how quickly one could recognize the sullied version.

Byrne climbed number 90's outside ladder. From a vantage point over the roof he could see the French Renaissance building of city hall growing in the distance with flags aflutter at several cornices surrounding the spire at its middle where a statue of William Penn stood impossibly high in the sky.

When the train pulled slowly into Philadelphia's center city stop at Broad Street, Harris jumped down and gave Byrne a hand signal to do the same.

They oversaw the uncoupling of Flagler's car and its positioning on a side rail where it would sit alone like some elegant museum piece while the smoke and ash and soot of the rest of the rail yard swirled round it.

Byrne stared wide-eyed at the grand towers of the Masonic Temple across the wide street.

"The exterior you're looking at is built of Cape Ann syenite, which takes its name from Syne in Upper Egypt, where it was quarried for monuments by the ancient Egyptians," a deep voice said. Byrne turned to see the man called Faustus standing just behind him, worrying on a pair of calfskin gloves. "The other sides are of Fox Island granite from the coast of Maine. Each stone, in accordance with Masonic tradition, was cut, squared, marked and numbered at the quarries and brought here ready for use."

"Is that so?" Byrne said, turning his head back to the Temple but admonishing himself for not detecting the man's presence earlier, "Mr. Faustus."

Despite the use of his name by a complete stranger, the elderly man did not miss a beat.

"Amadeus Faustus," he said, extending his gloved hand. Byrne shook it. "She was dedicated on Friday, September 26, 1873," Faustus continued. "The eighty-seventh anniversary of the independence of The Grand Lodge of Free and Accepted Masons of Pennsylvania."

This time Byrne looked directly in the man's light gray eyes, holding them. Was this the pitch of recruitment that Harris had warned him against?

"Thank you, sir. I will not forget," he said.

Faustus did not disengage his look. He reached into his vest pocket.

"I have no doubt of that, young man," he said and flipped a large coin into the air in Byrne's direction. Byrne snatched the object with a movement and speed like that of a snake strike. His reaction was habit, formed from hours of practice at a game he and Danny had perfected. Since they'd been kids on the street they'd passed idle time by positioning three coins on their forearms and then in a motion tossed all three into the air in front of them. The goal was to snatch all three out of the air, individually with separate strikes of the hand, palm down, before the last coin touched the ground. They'd been working on four coins when Danny left New York.

Byrne turned the coin in his hand and slipped it into his pocket.

"Not going to bite it to test its quality?" Faustus said, passing him in the direction of the entryway to the Temple.

"No sir," Byrne said. "That would be crass." He heard a sharp whistle from the direction of number 90 and hustled back to Harris' side.

"Mr. Flagler will need you to escort him to a business meeting, lad, while I accompany the missus to Wanamaker's," Harris said. They squared their shoulders in the direction of the departing Faustus, watching after him. Byrne showed the detective the coin the old man had tossed to him.

"I don't recognize it," Byrne said. "Worth anything?"

Harris looked at the markings on the metal and laughed.

"Not a penny," he said. "It's an old Confederate fifty-cent piece re-strike, lad. Not worth the metal it's stamped on. Useless, just like the man who gave it to ye."

CHAPTER SIX

BY MID MORNING THERE WERE MORE white people in the Styx than had ever set foot there at one time.

Mr. Wayne T. Pearson, the manager of The Poinciana and the Breakers, had arrived with his assistant. At first he'd simply been riled by the lack of a consistent staff at the hotels as the Negro workers had begun taking turns surveying their burned homes and sifting through the ashes for anything they could salvage. But when reports that the body of a man, a white man, had been found in the debris, Pearson was compelled to investigate. The fire had now become an urgent matter of rumor control.

Since it was his wagon being used to transport the black workers, Mr. Carroll, the head liveryman, was also there. Thorn Martin had relayed to him word of the white man's body, and that news, as well as blatant curiosity, had pulled him to the place as well. And then there was Miss McAdams, who had not left Ida May Fleury's side.

When Mr. Pearson arrived, the rest of the group was still standing near the rear of Shantice Carver's burned out shack, and they parted as if his substantial chin were the prow of boat.

Pearson did not say a word, only reading the eyes of the gathered people who glanced back at a flame-darkened lean-to. It was indication enough where the focus of the day lay. He stepped beyond the gathering and looked down on the corpse of the dead man. The body was stretched out on a platform of wood and protected to a degree by the lean-to roof that had obviously been used to store kindling and firewood. Pearson surprised the onlookers by going down on his haunches to get a better view. His assistant initially tried to follow suit but blanched at something—the look of the dead man's partially seared face or maybe the smell of burned flesh—and quickly abandoned his boss for a nearby tree trunk on which to retch. Pearson did not react. He was an older man and had seen battle in the Civil War as a teenager. Dreams and visions had visited him many times since. This experience was a mild dose of death.

Before him lay a man who appeared to be in his late twenties, broad of shoulder and tall, probably five-feet, nine-inches. The body was dressed in a dark-colored blouse, possibly of some kind of linen or even silk that appeared to have actually melted in spots and adhered to the man's skin. His trousers were of a style befitting an evening suit. His shoes were definitely made for a more formal affair than one this place might offer. Despite the disfiguring burns to the man's face, Pearson could see high cheekbones and remnants of a mustache that was indeed partially wrapped around a roll of singed U.S. paper currency protruding from the corpse's mouth. Pearson was unable to determine the denomination of the bills. Some six inches below that, where the dead man's Adam's apple should have been, was a blackened hole. Though his past experiences had been with wounds created by musket balls, Pearson had no trouble discerning that a bullet had been fired into the man's throat.

The manager finally stood and stepped back to give the site a more thoughtful survey, noting the near total destruction of anything flammable, including the four walls of the nearby shack. He took a folding knife from his pocket, approached the corner of the lean-to and took a deep carving from the wood and examined it. As he suspected, the wood, probably salvaged from some shipwreck or washed up on the beach from a floundering barge, was Dade County Pine, a wood known to be so hard and strong that it was nearly impossible to drive an iron nail through it. The wood's properties also made it impervious to only the hottest of flame, and it had indeed sheltered the dead man's body instead of hastening its total consummation by fire.

"Does anyone recognize this poor soul?" Pearson finally asked aloud, looking specifically at the livery supervisor and young Martin and then at his own assistant. "Percival? Step up here and take a look."

The assistant hesitated at the request and only jerked his knee as if his foot was railroad spiked into the dirt.

"For God's sake, son, it isn't diseased, it's only dead," Pearson said, and the younger man finally did manage to take a closer look but only shook his head in the negative and then backed off.

"Has anyone gone across the lake to inform the sheriff?" Pearson then said, again looking only at the white people in attendance.

"Uh, I believe, sir, everyone was waiting on you, sir," Mr. Carroll said.

"Well, I am not the coroner, Mr. Carroll. I am only a hotel manager. I suggest you go fetch Sheriff Cox and let him do his job, and as for the rest of you, we have guests at The Poinciana and Breakers who need not know anything of this." He finally eyeballed the Negro members of the group. "And should I find that those vacationers have heard of the details of this incident then I will surely know from whose mouths those details came."

All of the workers were now nodding their bowed heads under their manager's baleful eye and starting to take small, nearly imperceptible steps away from the space as if Pearson was wrong about the diseased nature of the scene.

"Meantime, I do commend you, Mizz Fluery, for your impromptu scheduling in the face of this adversity, but we do have a hotel to run.

"And Mr. Carroll, I do suggest that after summoning Sheriff Cox, you make sure that nothing, and I do mean nothing, changes here before he arrives."

The manager then turned on his heel and stepped over to Miss McAdams, offering her his crooked arm.

"You, Miss, may return with me in my carriage," he said, with a look that was not meant to be challenged.

The ride to the hotel was made in silence. Pearson and Marjory McAdams sat in back, looking out opposite sides of the carriage while the manager's assistant sat up with the driver. When they reached the turn to the Breakers' entrance, the assistant glanced over his shoulder for instruction. With a flip of his wrist Pearson indicated they veer right to The Royal Poinciana. Before protesting that her accommodations were in the beachside hotel, Marjory caught herself and kept her lips sealed. She'd been in trouble before when she was discovered doing something "untoward" and knew it was useless to react to anyone other than her father.

She sat back in the carriage with her hands folded in her lap and stared out at the meticulous landscaping of hotel grounds. It was now nearing noontime and the temperature had risen to the midseventies. The breeze from the ocean had also increased, and a scent of salt tinged the air. Couples were out walking along the wide, crushed-stone avenue, parasols raised against the sun. Others were bicycling toward the ocean. It was a quaint policy that no other vehicles were allowed on Flagler's hotel properties, certainly not the motorized kind that some of the wealthy guests from the north had recently been infatuated with. When Flagler's train pulled across the lake bridge to deliver his guests to what was now the largest resort hotel in the world, the noise of machines was something the oil tycoon's influential friends would not be bothered by. As an accommodation, guests moving about the island could be ushered any distance in the hotel's "Afromobiles." This contraption married a bicycle to a large wicker chair inside which guests could ride while a valet peddled from behind, taking them to any destination or simply for an hour's ride about the property. These conveyances were publicized as Afromobiles because most of the valets were Negro men.

As they passed three of these, Marjory looked carefully at the drivers, trying to discern from the look on their faces whether they knew what they had lost in the fire or were concerned over where they would sleep tonight. But their looks were as passive and unemotional as if they themselves were some part of the machinery they propelled. Marjory turned her eye to the rows of coconut palms that gracefully lined the avenue. Only the tuned ear heard the dead fronds in the tops, dried and scratching in the wind. She counted them, trying to distract herself from imagining the destination Mr. Pearson had in mind and in order to keep her mouth from getting her deeper into trouble. Instead, she speculated on who might identify the body now lying in the Styx, awaiting the sheriff, whose reputation preceded him as a man who was iron-handed when it came to keeping the sometimes boisterous rail workers in line during their off hours on the mainland and also making sure nothing that contained a whiff of illegality or violence should cross Lake Worth onto Palm Beach Island's fantasy getaway. She'd met the sheriff once, at a social luncheon, and he struck her as someone as false and vulgar as the cheap cologne he wore at midday.

When they finally pulled into a turnabout at the rear of the massive Poinciana, a livery boy took the horses by their bridles and a valet helped Marjory and Pearson down. In the side yards off to the north, Marjory could see a small gathering of ladies and gentlemen watching what could only be Roseann Birch, in full Victorian skirt and in full swing, hammering a golf ball out into an open field from a tee specifically built for the driving range. Roseann, a stout and irrepressible woman in her fifties, was the wife of an extremely rich banker in New York City, and Marjory had seen her harrumph and flick off any man who questioned her desire or participation in any activity at the hotel, be it golf, tennis, competitive swimming in the salt water pool or even skeet shooting.

"Men are simply boys with toys. The only deadly sports I stay away from are politics and real estate," she was famously known as saying aloud in mixed social settings, usually followed by a single-breath downing of a mint julep and an eye that challenged any man to match her estimable ability to consume alcohol.

Marjory followed Pearson's lead up the marbled stairs. As they crossed the expanse of the hotel's grand lobby Pearson's heels clacked over the inlaid Italian tile and every employee and nearly every guest tipped their heads in deference to the manager and half again as many made notice of Marjory. The men that she knew through introductions by her father indeed made it a point to touch the brims off their boaters and greet her by name as they passed. She greeted them by name if she remembered and by a subtle smile if she did not. Some of the newer guests were gaping up at the ornate frescos on the ceilings or at the arrangements of bright orange bird-of-paradise flowers shooting erotically from their boat-shaped cocoons and accented with their deep-blue tongues. The new arrivals always tickled Marjory in their awe of Florida's surprises, unique regardless of the guests' moneyed stations or wealth of travel experience.

At the front desk Pearson simply laid his hand on the polished onyx countertop and a sheave of telegraphs and messages were placed into his palm. He moved on without glancing at them. Even though the manager had still not vocally indicated their destination, a bit rude by most standards, Marjory refused to ask, but she could tell by the direction through the hotel and past the open lounges that they were headed toward Pearson's office.

At the oak door of the manager's suite, Pearson acted the gentleman, opening it and allowing her to enter first. He employed no secretary, passed through the outer office without breaking stride, again opened the door to his inner sanctum for Marjory, but stopped his assistant with a single glance and closed the door behind him. Marjory glanced back at the gesture and set her jaw. In mixed company, most especially a man with an unrelated woman, a door closed in private was an unusual occurrence.

"Please, sit, Miss McAdams," Pearson said, moving around to the business side of his massive desk. Marjory remained standing, turning away to face the fireplace. The hearth was cold and whisked clean of any ash. It was winter, but rarely did the temperature fall low enough for a fire, especially not in an office that would only be used during the daytime. She glanced at the photographs and framed certificates that lined the mantel. They all had to do with the building of the Royal Poinciana. None held any hint of the personal Mr. Pearson.

"I have here, Miss McAdams, a telegram from your father."

She turned at the pronouncement.

Pearson slid the typed paper across his desk, the surface of which was immaculately clean and without a single other object on its polished surface.

"He has asked that you remain in your suite at the beach hotel and await his arrival tomorrow on the afternoon train. He asks also that you refrain from any further contact with the situation in the Styx and not to speak of it to any of the other guests."

Marjory stepped across the room and laid her fingertips on the stiff paper of the telegram. She knew that the Florida East Coast rail stations each had telegraph offices and that messages were delivered twice daily, a staple for the businessmen clientele at the hotel, who were convinced they could not be out of touch with their various holdings in New York and elsewhere during their travels.

She picked up the telegram and without reading it slipped the paper into her pocket.

"Are you in the habit of reading everyone's correspondence before delivering it, Mr. Pearson?" she said, knowing she was on thin ice with the manager. But maybe that's what one does in Florida where there is no ice, she thought, dismissing the gravity of her disrespectful tone.

Instead of becoming angry, Pearson showed no emotion.

"Yes," he said, and Marjory swore she saw the slightest sign of a grin at the corner of his mouth.

The statement caught her speechless. The brazen possibilities, as well as the potential opportunities of such actions by the manager, only began to form in her head.

"I shall make sure that my father is aware of the policy," was the only retort she could form.

"I'm sure the information will be moot," Pearson said. "As it is he who instructed me to the policy when I was hired for this position."

Unlike with her father and many of his friends, Marjory couldn't tell whether this man was lying. He kept his gray eyes as blank and unreadable as a washed slate.

"You may go," he finally said.

She formed a vitriolic response behind her tongue, but held it. She spun on one heel and walked ever so carefully toward the door but stopped and again faced the desk.

"Did you recognize him, Mr. Pearson?" she said. "The dead man?"

The manager raised his head and looked up through his eyebrows, but hesitated for only a beat.

"You were there, Miss McAdams, when I asked if anyone recognized the unfortunate soul."

"Yes," she said. "You asked if anyone else recognized him, Mr. Pearson. But you didn't say whether you did."

There was now a twitch in the manager's cheek. She had perhaps gone too far.

"You may go," he repeated.

Marjory pinched both sides of her skirt and performed a slight curtsey.

"Yes, sir," she said, and stepped out of the office. Only later did she wonder where the southern accent of her "Yeas sir" had come from. She was sure that it came across as if she were a slave obeying the demands of the plantation owner. She would be in even deeper trouble with her father if that indiscretion was also communicated.

Marjory made her way outside onto the hotel's wide colonnade, a broad, covered porch lined with rocking chairs that overlooked the emerald-green yards. There were a few women in the chairs, dressed in their Victorian finery, chatting side-by-side or simply working their embroidery in their laps while enjoying the breeze. Two men in seersucker suits, straw boaters and the white shoes typical of dressed-down vacationers smoked cigars and talked in low voices near one of the white columns. But most of the hotel guests were in the distance in the Coconut Grove, seated at linen-covered tables under the shade of the palms. The hotel orchestra was playing. Marjory could make out the strains of a Sousa march, "The Belle of Chicago" or "The Bride Elect," she could never tell the difference. She moved to an isolated spot along the rail and took the telegraph from her pocket.

my dear Marjory...arriving noon train Wednesday 13...please, please behave and remain charming...will call on you at beach suite in due time to discuss recent matter...until then hold your own counsel...pp.

Confined to my suite and ordered not to speak to any of the guests of the burning of the Styx and the death of a white gentleman found with a roll of money in his mouth indeed, she thought. It says no such thing! Pearson's reading of the telegram was typical of a military man's ciphering, strict and strident, black and white. It's a wonder the north won the war at all with such men at the switch.

Her father was asking for her best manners because with him gone she was the only representative of the family on site. Rather than banning her from discussing the situation, her father knew of her inherent inquisitiveness and no doubt wanted to speak with her about the events to gain as much knowledge firsthand before others in his employ.

That was a far stretch from the angered and distressed accounting offered by Pearson. The true meaning of the message was only reinforced by the signature, pp, which was the endearing term "Pa Pa" that she had used with her father since childhood.

Marjory tucked the telegram back into her skirts and looked out onto the grounds. The man was after all very well regarded by her father and Mr. Flagler himself. She closed her eyes. Asking him out loud if he'd recognized the dead man! My God, girl, what were you thinking? Still, he had not confirmed nor denied, had he? She set back her emotions and in her head took account of what she'd witnessed at the Styx. In her mind's eye she marked off the length of the lean-to, where the heels of the corpse lay, then the head. She was astonished that the fire hadn't consumed the entire mess. She had seen the singed mustache, but hadn't dared to look closely at the face, burned as it was. She squeezed her eyes tighter.

It would be best at this point to describe the man and the situation to her father when he arrived tomorrow in simple, vague terms. Was it possible that he would recognize the victim? She didn't think so. Such a man was not the kind her father would have been acquainted with.

Marjory still had her eyes closed when the orchestra struck the opening chords of "After the Ball" and she opened them and looked out toward Coconut Grove. Maurice, the band's conductor, was certainly dancing at his own boundaries, she thought, by playing the popular *Tin Pan Alley* tune. Then her eye was caught by a dark knot of men moving up the walkway toward the hotel entrance.

There were three, but only one mattered. He was the shortest of the group but the most imposing. The others were as accessories, flanking out from the substantial girth of Sheriff Maxwell Cox. No one, Marjory thought, would have to second-guess the identity of the notorious sheriff after a single glance. Cox was an imposing keg of a man, almost inhumanly broad in the chest with muscled arms and back curving down from his thick shoulders like oak slats on a barrel. His trunklike legs and hips moved as one, creating a rolling motion, and she couldn't help think that if he fell he would surely continue to roll like a massive bowling ball to his destination. Marjory involuntarily put the tips of her fingers to her lips to stifle a laugh. Sheriff Cox was not a man to take as a joke.

She continued to watch the sheriff and his dark-suited entourage move up the walkway to the main entrance of the hotel. She had no doubt that their destination was the very office she'd just left. Cox was the leading law enforcement officer in all of Dade County, which encompassed everything on the east coast from Sebastian Inlet at the north boundary to the new village of Miami to the south. The sheriff had only recently been spending more and more time in West Palm Beach, where money and influence was flowing in on Flagler's coattails. Pearson's orders to bring him to the island had been followed with haste and now the big man was here to set things straight. Cox's southern past came with a reputation of being particularly harsh when it came to Florida's migrant population, and the very whisper of a white man found dead in a Negro community would have inspired him to inject his authority without wasting time.

Marjory watched the procession and caught the lyrics of the tune being played for those at tea in the grove, most of whom were no doubt oblivious of the burning of an entire community only a couple of miles from their afternoon merriment:

After the ball is over, after the break of morn, After the dancers leaving, after the stars are gone, Many a heart is aching, if you could read them all— Many the hopes that have vanished after the ball.

CHAPTER SEVEN

IT WAS THE DARKNESS THAT STUNNED Michael Byrne, kept him awake and outside on the platform of the caboose staring at the flat blackness of a moonless night. He had never encountered such a lack of light, a total void like a black painted panel of nothingness for miles and miles at a time. He could only imagine the silence because the train's own mechanical huffing and grinding and clacking overwhelmed all else, but he knew it was out there in that blackness. That unchecked silence made him think of that barroom conundrum: if a tree falls in the woods and no one is there to hear it, does it make a sound? He could also only imagine the lack of movement since he stood on this platform and its constant rocking, back and forth, over the uneven and frequently dipping rails. But out there, he could see no tilt or rumble, push or shove, rise or fall. He might have been mesmerized. He might have even been a bit scared. But he wasn't sleeping. This moving landscape was too strange and awesome for a young man born in the constant sidewalk swirl, cacophonic sound and unavoidable light of the city.

After Henry Flagler's business meeting in Philadelphia and after his wife's numerous boxes and cartons and purchases from Wanamaker's were loaded, their private car was moved back onto a main track and switched onto yet another southbound train.

"This is one of Mr. Flagler's own FEC trains," Harris said. "Straight to Jacksonville now, lad, no stopping unless Mr. Flagler himself asks."

When they hit Washington, D.C., Byrne's view was restricted to what he could see when the train stopped briefly to take on passengers at the Pennsylvania railroad station at the base of Capitol Hill. Still in the late afternoon light, he could see the glowing white dome of the Capitol Building to the east and the towering Washington Monument to the west. He recalled a night at McSorely's when a traveler described the monument as a giant spear shooting straight up into the sky, the tallest structure in the world, although some equally drunk Frenchman argued there was a taller tower in Paris that had been built for the World's Fair. After seeing the marble shaft in the distance, Byrne would now have to side with the traveler, but that night he and the boys had a laugh when the man and Frenchy got into a fistfight over the whole affair and ended up out on Seventh Street lying in a gutter of frozen horse urine, which no one would argue was the lowest point in the United States.

The train rolled south for the rest of the evening and night. Byrne and Harris took turns walking the cars, again running surveillance on new passengers. "Puttin' 'em in the iron sites," Harris called it. But there was no one of interest. Another family, this time with the head of household in attendance, a businessman from D.C. whose shrewish wife stared at the side of her husband's face when another woman passenger walked through ahead of Byrne to see whether he would look up from the papers he was reading. Two new men traveling alone had taken places in the club car. One was working at a flask in his coat pocket, surreptitiously hitting at the neck of the bottle. He'd be unconscious before eight o'clock, Byrne determined.

Mr. Faustus had reboarded. He winked once when Byrne passed through the sitting car. But Byrne avoided the subtle invitation to stop and talk, albeit with great reluctance. There was something about the old man's interest in him that was palpable, or maybe he tested everyone he met on the train. Perhaps he'd even met Danny. Byrne wanted to pick the old man's brain, find out more on his own rather than judge the man based only on Harris' cryptic appraisal. But for now he would wait, as the sergeant had warned. Instead Byrne moved along and chose the "binder boys" as his intelligence target.

"Evenin', boy'os," he said to the group and slid into a seat without asking.

The three glanced at one another and then the oldest looking of the team slid a bit over and said: "Free country, mate."

"You're on from New York, eh?" Byrne said, using his accent from the street, not kissing up, but unashamedly trying to take advantage of a connection based on Harris' information.

"Brewer's Row in Bushwick," said one. He was German-looking. Byrne checked his hands, small and uncalloused, his eyes were clear and smart under high cheekbones. Might be the smartest of the bunch, he thought.

"Cherry Hill," said the swarthier one. Italian, Byrne guessed. Scar on his cheek, possibly from a knife cut. His were shifting eyes, working his peripheral vision, expecting someone to come up behind him in a strange place.

The older one was looking at his mates, Byrne figured he was calculating his own answer. He was displaying an easy, knowledgeable air—strike up conversation with a stranger without a problem, feel them out for something to take advantage of. He'd be the one calling marks in off the street, reeling in the rubes for a game of three-card or into the brothel for a turn. He'd be the one most like Danny.

"Tenderloin, my friend," he finally said like he'd pinned a flower in his lapel. "And you?"

"Gas House District," Byrne said and then made careful eye contact with each one of the men. It might have been a declaration of battle if the conversation and demarcation of neighborhoods had been taking place on the streets of New York. But the need for piss-marking their territory was absent here on a train to a place called Florida. They all had something in common, an adventure into an unknown where none of them had been before and had no allies.

"A Pinkerton from the Gas House," the older one said, looking down at Byrne's shoes.

"That obvious?" he said, not bothering to dispute the fact.

"Them brogans are like a badge, Pinkerton," he said. "Anybody with a brain on the street knows that, my friend."

"That they would, my Tenderloin friend," Byrne said, straightening out his legs, crossing his ankles out in the aisle and getting comfortable. "So boy'os," he said. "Tell me about your game."

"Don't tell me a Lower East Side Pinkerton needs a course on three-card Monte," the smart one said.

Byrne crinkled up a grin at the side of his face. "Wouldn't tell you that, my friend. It's not the card game I'm unfamiliar with," he said, nodding at the leather briefcases tucked beside each one. "It's the real estate business."

The Italian's hand was the first to go to his case, almost unconsciously placing his palm across the flap. Byrne guessed him to be the poorest of the lot and most likely to be one of those Harris had said would have borrowed the investment money from his family and friends to make a killing in sunny Florida.

"I'm not interested in the money, boy'os," Byrne said, raising his palms toward them. "Only interested in the game."

The older one eyed him. "Never trust an Irishman who says he's not interested in the money," he said and then let his own grin take a corner of his face.

"Indeed," Byrne said and they smiled together and some sort of curbside trust was entered into.

"The premise ain't much different from playin' the streets," Tenderloin said. "Buy somethin' from the market down on Watts and then run it up Broadway and sell it as new for a profit before the yuks up there seen it."

Byrne nodded. He and Danny had done the same thing as boys, snatching up new cloth their mother had acquired and running it up to a seamstress in mid-Manhattan where they got twice the price.

"The market for land is brand new and strong as hell down in Florida. The place is near empty, land spreadin' out like a green jungle and just waitin' for people to come work it or live on it," the older one continued.

"Not much different than north Manhattan Island when your old da, and mine, got to America, right?"

Byrne started to react to the mention of his "old da" but since the man from the Tenderloin had tossed his own family into the mix, he let it go as an unintended slur.

"You need money to make money, right, Pinkerton? So you use what money you have and buy up a chunk of land that looks like it's gonna be in the center of town in due time, and believe me, the times run damn fast down in Florida.

"My first trip down, Palm Beach was a pimple on me mum's ass. Now the bloody place has a palace on the shore and it's spillin' across the lake to what they're callin' West Palm Beach. The county surveyor already wacked the place out into mapped lots and streets while it was still farmland. Sound familiar?"

Tenderloin nodded to his companion from Bushwick.

"Just like Brooklyn," he said.

"Right-O," said Tenderloin. "And while the Vanderbilts got the east shore line for their mansions early, the rest of 'em got the Cross Roads."

Byrne sat back and watched the trio's eyes, especially those of the Italian. Were they optimistic boys, or angry ones? He knew that the man he was paid to be guarding was not only considered an oil magnate and a railway magnate, but the phrase "robber baron" had also been used to describe him. Flagler had built his destination hotels down the east coast of Florida at a time when there wasn't a damn thing south of Jacksonville.

"Not that you've got anything against the ones first in line," Byrne said, not even attempting to be coy. The man from the Tenderloin began to laugh.

"Hell no, Pinkerton. We ain't got nothin' but admiration for your boss Mr. Flagler back there in car ninety." He then leaned in conspiratorially. "People bigger'n us been following the old gent around for years, tryin' to figure where he's going next so's they could jump up the price of their land or buy it out before the mighty Flagler arrives.

"Fact is, the old man did it himself the same way. Promised to take his railroad all the way to Miami, he did. Even the state legislature knew money and progress would follow. They gave him eight thousand acres of right of way for every mile of track the old fella built. He'll have millions of acres free of charge by the time he's through."

Numbers had never been Byrne's strong suit, but he was no fool. And he now realized his assessment of the shyster from the Tenderloin district was far too low. The man had done his homework.

"Don't matter who's first," he said. "There's plenty of Florida to buy and sell. The railroad and new hotels just make it easier for the pigeons to follow, if you get my drift. No, Pinkerton, we got no quarrel with old Henry, long shall he live."

Tenderloin reached into his jacket for a small flask, a gesture followed by the other two, and the tiny mob tossed back a toast.

"It's not the likes of us small-timers you've got to worry about, Pinkerton," he said. "It's the big players like the high falutin' Mr. Faustus up there in the smoking room you should have your eye on. He's more of a danger than any of us will ever be. Listenin' to his Peter Funk sermons on the right way to live will lead ya to doin' nothing but starvin' to death while he builds his church on your back." Tenderloin bobbed his head once, statement served. Conversation ended.

Byrne had risen then and unconsciously slipped his hand into his pocket where his fingertips found the confederate coin. He wasn't worried about Faustus quite yet. He'd heard his brother do the carny barker's routine and the preacher's harangue and the bait-and-switch patter enough to spot a puller-in. No, Faustus would be one to watch, but right now he figured he'd ingratiated himself enough with these lads to ask his question:

"So, you boy'os ever run across a man name of Danny Byrne?"

The three looked again at one another. Admitting to knowing a man who wasn't present to a Pinkerton was not something any one of them would do lightly. It would be akin to ratting someone out on the streets, and it always stunk of trouble that could come back on you.

"About my size," Byrne pressed on. "Bit more red in his hair and a few years older."

The one from the Tenderloin studied Byrne's face with even more intensity than he already had.

"People change their names down in Florida," he finally said.

"Aye, and elsewhere," Byrne replied and added a grin.

They all nodded in ascent.

Byrne tipped his head goodnight to the group.

"Any time," said Tenderloin, extending his hand. "Gerald Haney."

Byrne took the hand and shook it. "Michael Byrne."

"Oh, then it's a relative you're lookin' for," the binder boy said, changing his tone a bit, but still wary, like he was gathering his own intelligence.

"My brother," Byrne admitted, not knowing why he suddenly felt he'd been too forthcoming.

"Well then, we'll keep an eye out," said Tenderloin and tipped his own chin goodnight.

Now, from the platform of the caboose, Byrne looked out on the matte of blackness behind them and had the overwhelming feeling that the train he was on was the only living thing in the night, roaring through an uneasy nothingness. It was an odd, sliding community, he thought, filled with people strange and familiar at the same time. When he woke in the morning light he would be in Florida, land of sunshine and honey, he'd been told. But somehow he was building an increasing doubt of that description.

"Jacksonviiiilllle. Jacksonville!" the voice called out, penetrating Michael Byrne's head and causing him to jolt up off the lower cot and reach for his baton, which was always tucked beside him. The caboose was empty but for the sunlight streaking in through the side windows. The other train workers were long gone, including Harris, who had the morning shift anyway, but Byrne was still surprised that he had slept through the dawn. He swung his legs over the edge of the cot, and when his feet hit the deck, he felt the purr of the machine beneath him. Through the soles of his feet, he could feel the vibration of the engine, like the deep snore of a large animal, but no movement. They'd come to a full stop, and he couldn't believe he hadn't awakened.

He dressed quickly and poured himself a cup of coffee that Harris must have made on the small wood stove. It was still hot, but he found himself looking into the mug, confused by the lack of steam and the new feel of sweat filming on his face. He turned to one of the sliding side windows and found it wide open. Even before he opened the rear door, he noticed the collection of coats still hanging on the hook and then stepped through to the platform. The rail station was relatively small, a single track and two turnouts. He found it curious to see the remnants of another set of tracks running parallel that were smaller in width and definitely of a different gauge. He leaned out over one side and took in the small wooden station building and the plank platform that appeared aged in a way that brought dry bones to mind. He found himself squinting in the too bright light and used one hand to shade his eyes and check the position of the sun. It was barely fifteen degrees up in the sky so it couldn't have been past nine in the morning, but the orb seemed far too close to be natural. He spotted a handful of workers wheeling a cargo of crates and barrels from a loading dock and noted that all of the men were wearing sleeveless shirts and hats darkly stained with sweat. He found himself again wiping his own damp forehead with the back of his hand and whispered: "Jaysus, it's hotter than Hades."

Byrne was just taking a deep breath of the heated, new-tasting air when he heard Harris calling his name from the interior of the caboose.

"Rise and shine, lad. You've got fifteen minutes to get ready for a bit of a side trip." They nearly collided at the back door. "Mr. Flagler has decided to take an excursion to Jacksonville Beach with some of his business friends and interested passengers, and you'll be needin' to go along."

"Right," said Byrne, starting to cough on the lungful of moist air.

Harris was smiling.

"Aye, bit of a new climate for you, boy. But you'll get used to it. Some folks pay a pretty penny to come down here and breath this stuff, and I'm givin' you the chance to sample the best of it if you'll just get your arse in gear."

"Right," Byrne said again, already moving about the cabin, pulling a cake of shaving soap and his sharp knife from the sheath on his calf.

"Mr. Flagler wants to take a look at just what the new spur he built to the beachfront has bought him," Harris said, pouring himself a cup of coffee from the metal pot. "You'll be ridin' a work train over that's meant to haul in material from the coal and lumber docks. The cars should be empty, but there's still a gang of state convicts the company leased to do the hard haulin' and they ain't exactly a friendly bunch. I don't want the boss out there without one of us nearby just in case somebody gets pissy, mind you."

"Right," Byrne said a third time, buttoning his shirt and slipping on his suspenders. He rinsed off the knife and slipped it back in the sheath, rolling his pants leg back over it, and then reached for his coat.

"I wouldn't suggest takin' that," Harris said, that know-it-all grin once again coming to his face.

Byrne removed the telescoping baton from inside the coat and slipped it down into his hip pocket. As they started out the door Harris stopped, reached up into a baggage rack, brought down a small cloth jockey cap and handed it to Byrne.

"Only a fool walks around in the Florida sun without a hat, m'boy," Harris said and continued out the door.

Byrne noticed the immediate advantage in having a brim to pull down and shade his eyes. He'd never experienced such sunlight: intense, clear and blinding if one didn't keep it from glancing directly off the face. He scanned the surrounding rail yard. It seemed nearly as busy as that of the Philadelphia stop but in a different manner. Here, building material and supplies were flowing. Flat cars were being stacked with lumber and men wheeled crates up ramps into the adjoining box cars. The heated air was pungent with the odor of sawdust and raw earth and sweat. Byrne was standing near Flagler's car and stepped closer to number 90 when he heard movement at the door. Without forethought he inadvertently moved into the shade created by the train car and felt the temperature of his exposed skin immediately start to cool. "Only a fool stands in the direct sun when there is shade available," he whispered under his breath. Harris could have taught him more than just the hat trick.

When Mr. Flagler finally appeared in the doorway, he was wearing a suit of light wool including a collar shirt and tie and an odd pair of darkly shaded spectacles of the likes Byrne had never seen. Flagler stepped down spryly and began immediately across the station decking headed south. He was, Byrne would soon learn, in business mode, his bearing straight and purposeful, his eyes set straight ahead but still absorbing all around him. Byrne fell in behind the man and shortly realized that, like some kind of pied piper, Flagler began to draw suited men from the offices and doorways, who were seemingly trying to draw his notice or simply gather some of the great man's luck or brilliance by trailing in his wake. The gathering made Byrne nervous and he slid his hand down in his pocket where he fingered the metal baton. But the group kept their distance, greeting Flagler with good humor and welcomes. They all appeared to know his destination and no one stepped out in front of the man's path. After crossing thirty yards of limestone rail yard, the entourage approached another set of tracks where an engine with only two cars attached sat waiting. Byrne could see from the grime and soot, with which he was intimately familiar, that this was a working engine and looked odd hauling the clean passenger cars that appeared to have been hastily brought on line for the occasion. Flagler was greeted by a man in a business suit who looked uncomfortable in the getup, and Byrne heard him introduced as the shipping yard manager. Flagler shook the man's hand in a friendly manner and smiled, the first time Byrne had seen him do so, and the men all round seemed to physically relax. But when the manager motioned for Mr. Flagler to be the first to board the first car, Byrne stepped up to his boss's side.

"If I may be allowed, sir?" he said.

If the railway baron was caught unawares he showed no sign, only coolly raising one white eyebrow before responding:

"I do not think it necessary, this being my own property, Mr. Byrne. Yet it is your job, I suppose."

"Yes, sir," Byrne said and then clambered up the steps and went swiftly but efficiently through the rail car, eyeing every possible hiding place and corner before returning and then dropping again to Flagler's side. The man simply raised his eyebrow again in question and then returned Byrne's nod as affirmation that it was safe to board. Byrne stood at the door stoically, but carefully memorized the dress and facial features of a dozen men and any lump or pull on their coats or the fabric of hips where gun or knife handles might be concealed as they climbed the stairs. The shipping manager was the last.

"Is there a reason, young Pinkerton, for such scrutiny?"

"Mr. Flagler is an important man," Byrne said dryly.

"No news in that, Pinkerton. And getting more important by the day I would venture."

"Board!" the manager yelled out toward the engineer in typical trainman's manner and stepped up into the car. Byrne let thirty feet pass and then grabbed the next car's metal banister and swung himself up onto the entire moving mass.

From the grated platform at the rear of the short train Byrne watched the city of Jacksonville spread out. Harris had told him the town was the southern terminus of all rail traffic before Flagler. He found it unimpressive—some brick buildings and facades, some stone-paved streets but curiously no street lights. Most of the place was dominated by wooden structures and wagon traffic and the rail yards. As they moved east, the view widened and he realized what was missing. The sunlight was unimpeded. Yes it was hot, he could feel the sweat under his vest move in a single trickle down between his shoulder blades and twice already he'd used the hat Harris had given him to mop his forehead. But he soon realized it was the air itself that seemed to glisten with a purity he had never experienced. The place was absent of the smoky haze that always hung in New York. He had once listened to a watchmaker at McSorely's talk about being fitted with a new pair of spectacles to correct his deteriorating eyesight. He described the new lenses as creating such "sharp, colorful and detailed vision that it was as if the entire world was reborn." A couple of the fellows at the bar asked to try them and only winced and became dizzied by the experiment. Now Byrne thought that this present view was what the watchmaker must have experienced. He doubted that anyone could wince at anything so crystal.

Soon Byrne felt the angle of the train change and he swung his torso out around the corner of the car to see that they were slowly mounting a bridge that spanned a river called the St. Johns. The small freight bridge was nothing to compare with the Williamsburg Bridge at home but neither was this river anything to compare with the East River. Byrne stared down into what was obviously water—he could plainly see small boats moving with the current. But he was confused to see that the shadows of those craft followed slightly behind with the angle of the sun. When he leaned over and checked the bridge supports below he witnessed the same phenomenon, shadows from the stanchions were stretched out from the base. He at first thought it was some sort of optical illusion until his staring determined that the shadows were actually rippling and he was finally convinced that the water itself was clear. The shadows were playing along the white bottom of the river itself. He had never seen water so clean.

Once over the bridge they picked up speed across what appeared to be a dry peninsula of scrub plants and low trees of a variety again foreign to Byrne. After some thirty minutes he heard the sound of the train whistle and felt the shift in momentum to slow. Again he leaned out to see ahead and was once again greeted by a sight unequaled. Now before them on the horizon was the Atlantic Ocean in a shade of blue-green Byrne had only seen in samples of the colored cloth his mother had once sewn in their tenement as piecework for other women's dresses. His neck began to ache as he held himself out over the railing, and in frustration he decided to climb the carriage ladder to the top of the train car so he might look forward and out on the view. From the higher point, with the wind in his face, Byrne was mesmerized. The vista of water changing color from cyan to turquoise to teal and then to steel blue out at the very edge of the earth was stunning. Along the shore was a foam line of cream and then the white of sand beach that made him squint at its brightness and think quickly of Flagler's odd looking shaded glasses.

The tracks became lined with loading platforms and tin-roofed storage sheds where stacks of lumber waited. Byrne noted the scent of fresh-cut wood, the bite of turpentine, but also something else that dominated and reminded him of the fish markets back home off Water Street.

His attention was quickly caught by a group of workers ahead. They were a gang of men sweating under the direct sun, hefting railway ties as part of a secondary track siding. All of them were dressed in worn and tattered gray trousers with a stripe in the leg seam. On their heads they all wore striped hats the kind of which Byrne did recognize. Prisoners. He had seen the same headwear on work crews from The Tombs. He looked now with more scrutiny at the edges of the group and finally spotted the guards: two men, standing easily to the east and west, both cradling rifles in their arms. Byrne quickly moved down off the roof, entered the car below and made his way to where Flagler was entertaining, or being entertained, by his business associates. The well-dressed men were standing loosely, their hands in their pockets or thumbs in their vests, all seemingly held in rapt attention by whatever Flagler was saying. The old man himself would speak a few sentences and then bend at the waist to look out the window and appraise whatever it was he could see. The train was moving slowly, and when Byrne also bent to look out the window he noted that not one of the working men looked up or took notice. The worlds of the men inside and out were a universe apart. It was not unlike the thousands of gaunt, starving faces Byrne watched and recorded every day of his life in the tenements of the Lower East Side and those nouveau riche he would later watch over as a barrier cop as they entered Delmonico's at Fifth Avenue and Twenty-sixth Street. He only pondered the feeling that his past seemed to be following him when the train began to slow further and the sense of the foundation in his feet shifted. He looked to the east to see that the engine was now moving out onto some kind of a pier, leaving land behind. He made a quick assessment and decided that with only those aboard to accompany him, Flagler would be safe. With the train starting to move out over the sea, Byrne stepped out onto the stair step and then jumped down onto the rocky ground.

With the sound of his feet sliding in the flint bed of the railway tracks, Byrne's sudden movement attracted the attention of one of the prison guards, who swung his rifle. Byrne raised one hand, tipped his hat politely and dusted his trousers with the other. With a quick glance at his clothing and shoes the guard became satisfied that no alarm was needed, nodded and turned back to the gang work. Byrne was pleased that the guard didn't bother with even a cursory questioning. He would have hated to admit he was intensely fearful of being out over water and his motivation for jumping from the train was not just because he thought Flagler was safe.

The train had stopped at the end of the pier and Byrne counted three ships that were lashed to the northern side of the dockage. Two were three-masted Clipper ships that must have measured some 130 feet in length. Their sails were down, and Byrne noted the davits built along Flagler's docks that were used to reach over and haul off the lengths of lumber being imported into the state to build not only Flagler's new hotels but also the commercial buildings and homes that cropped up around them. Byrne had seen the same type of sailing ships along the East and the Hudson Rivers that flanked New York. What he had not seen in New York was the vision he now took in from the south. The aqua water was even clearer and cleaner from this vantage point. He stared at the ribbon of white ground being brushed by the waves that led up to the low tangle of scrub brush. Considering the stacks of wood plank behind him, it seemed no surprise that trees would be afraid to grow anywhere near here. But it was the white ground that intrigued him, and against his better judgment to stay near Flagler's train, he moved down the embankment to the flat stretch leading to the water.

Byrne had seen sand before, used in concrete filler or mixed with mortar for brickwork. He had seen powder before, on the dressing tables at a brothel when he was part of a police raiding party in the Tenderloin district. He had never seen the two mixed, and that's what he found himself standing on. The sand was so fine he was at first afraid to step onto it. Finally he walked out several yards and then bent down and touched the ground as if to see whether it were real. He pinched the substance between his fingers and rubbed the white grain back and forth, feeling the texture. If he could have seen himself smile he would have been embarrassed at the childish wonder of it. He stood, wiped his fingertips on his dark trousers and moved farther out toward the sea. The foam of small breaking waves was sluicing up onto the sand and leaving it a shade or two darker but still the whiteness caused the water to look so clear and pure he could not help himself and he removed his brogans and socks, rolled his pants legs up over the sheath of his knife and stepped out into the water. The slickness of wet sand tickled the soles of his feet, like he'd stepped onto clay. The water was also warm, and he instantly thought of the heat that had smothered him when he first encountered it this morning but had been forgotten once the ocean came into sight. The breeze that came off the sea had cooled his sweat and taken the flush off his face. He looked down into a foot of crystal water, cleaner than anything that came from the spigots of the city, and without hesitation he bent and cupped a handful, tossed it into his face, then brought up another handful and started to drink. The gulp was halfway down his throat when he gagged; the raw taste caused him to spit the offending swallow out in a spray and sent him into a coughing jag.

"Jaysus!" he spat, and it was as if the smell he'd been puzzled by earlier was now in his mouth.

"Ha," came a bark of laughter from behind him, and Byrne spun about to see Faustus standing just above the tide mark in dry sand. "First time at the ocean, Mr. Byrne?" he called. "Oh, she does look glorious and pure doesn't she? Enough clear blue water to slake the thirst of an army. Especially inlanders who have never known a clear stream or lake they couldn't drink from."

Byrne was backing away from that water, licking his lips and spitting every three steps, trying to clear the taste from his mouth.

"Salt, my friend. Wonderful sea salt. Never been in salt water have you, landlubber?"

Byrne had not seen Faustus on the excursion train. How he'd made the journey over the river from the rail station was beyond him, but there he was, dressed in a cream-colored suit and wearing a straw boater. He had the same cane in his hand and was teasing the sand in front of him with the tip. Byrne made his way back to his socks and shoes, still within earshot of Faustus.

"Our boys from western Georgia and the mountains of Carolina had the same experience when the first regiments were driven to the sea. They were exhausted and scared and that first sight of clear, clean water made some of them so damned giddy they tossed themselves right in and started gulping to relieve their thirst," Faustus continued.

Byrne redressed his feet and remained quietly embarrassed.

"A belly full of salt water will give you the trots though, son."

"I will take your word for it, sir," Byrne said and there was an amusement in his voice now that came from his own self-deprecation. "Though I do remember my mother using a dose of it to wash out my mouth after losing a tooth or two."

Byrne stood and rolled down his pant legs only to find that the surf had gotten to the last four inches, leaving his cuffs wet and his knife sheath dark.

"So, Mr. Faustus, I didn't see you on the train. How did you come to find me here?"

"Believe me, young Pinkerton, there are more ways to get around this state than just on Mr. Flagler's trains. It is in fact one of the beauties of the place, that freedom of movement."

"I did notice that not everyone is free," Byrne said, nodding toward the loading docks and the convict labor group.

"Ah, of course you, being such an astute observer, would have seen the work crews in their high distinctive prison garb," Faustus said. "Hard to believe that a generation ago those Confederate uniforms were being worn by brave young men trying to save the South from just this kind of future.

"Yet I believe the Union armies had secured several large shipments of the clothing near the end of the war and finding it hard to sell them in that present market they simply doled them out to the states for convicts and beggars, neither of which group can be choosy."

"To the winners the spoils," Byrne said. It was a facetious statement—in Byrne's world it was smart-assed—but Faustus caught up on it.

"Like your employer, the winner," he said. Byrne stayed quiet. He did not argue matters of fact.

"Mr. Flagler obtains generous contracts with the state of Florida to lease the labor of convicts for the muscle it takes to build a railway. Those are just a few you saw. He employs them for one dollar and twenty-five cents a month. When he has to hire the few locals in these parts or culls laborers from your part of the country, Mr. Byrne, they are paid that much per day. It works out quite nicely for him, even though he does pay for their room and board of course, along with the salary of the guards. The man isn't some slave Satan."

If the information was meant to influence Byrne's perception of Flagler it was wasted on his ears. His mother had made less than a dollar and a quarter a month sewing piece work back home in their tenement apartment. He had seen rag pickers, the dregs of the dregs in New York, standing knee deep in refuse at dumpsites along the East River reaching in to find anything they could to salvage and resell on the streets. Convicts sweating through a day or a month's hard labor if only for food did not stir his compassion. No, his first thought was with the sometimes nefarious leanings of his brother, the fact that he didn't have to scour the group of criminals for a glimpse of Danny was a blessing, confirmed by the telegram in his pocket. His second thought was of the possible threat to his boss, and that pulled his attention from the ocean and sand to the pier and the sound of the train engine beginning to rumble and throttle up.

Byrne took one last look at the sea to the south.

"It is quite a sight," he said aloud but mostly to himself.

"There will be many more surprises along the way, young Pinkerton," Faustus said.

Byrne took a step in the direction of the pier. "You catching the train back, sir?"

"No. You go along Mr. Byrne. Each man to his master."

Byrne continued up the slight rise, thinking of a rejoinder, but when he turned again to Faustus, the man was simply gone.

When all returned to the rail depot and Mr. Flagler was securely returned to his private car, Byrne marched quickly to the caboose, hoping not to run into Harris. Flagler had said nothing of his Pinkerton detective rejoining his group wearing trousers that were wet to midcalf. There was no doubt in Byrne's mind that the observant rail baron had not missed the sight. But then Byrne was hired help. Now he just looked the part. He was climbing the steps of the car when Harris came around the corner. His sergeant met the discoloration of his new charge's pants legs at eye level.

"Ah, lad. Took a bit of a dip in the deep blue sea, did we?"

Byrne said nothing but could feel the heat rise in his face.

"Can't blame you, son. Hell of a sight for a tenement kid, eh? Didn't know such color existed on the planet myself when I took my first trip down here. We arrived late at night and the crew chief needed help with some security problem down at the oceanfront and I had to rub my eyes twice to believe what I was seeing.

"I'll tell you, boy. With a full moon shining on that beach what with all that whiteness, I thought it had snowed."

"It's a strange place, Mr. Harris," was all Byrne could think to say.

"That it is, son. So get yourself changed. There's a whiff in the air that Mr. Flagler's needed in Palm Beach as soon as we can get there," Harris waved what appeared to be a sheet of teletype in his hand. Whatever the message was, the sergeant did not share it and hustled away.

After he'd dressed, in the only other pair of pants he owned, Byrne went out onto the depot siding and found a patch of shade over a bench. There was a discarded newspaper on an unused luggage cart and he picked it up. The *Jacksonville Times Union.*

On the front page there was news from Washington of which he had no interest or knowledge. Something about trouble in Cuba, wherever that was. A piece about emerging conflict in Germany. On the inside pages there was a testimonial for Herbine, described as "the most perfect liver medicine and the greatest blood purifier."

Byrne had seen or heard the equal in New York City from corner criers or on store window announcements since he was a boy. But as he skimmed the pages a clump of unfamiliar words caught his eye:

Jacksonville is scheduled to have a triple hanging on Friday, August 7th.

He re-read the first sentence and then worked out the rest.

Governor Jennings has signed death warrants fixing that date for the execution of three murderers convicted in the circuit court for Duval County, and they have been forwarded to Sheriff John Price, of that county. The men are Frank Carter, convicted of the murder of Charlie Phillips on November 2; Frank Roberson, convicted of the murder of James Smith on October 26. All of the murders, of course, were committed in Duval County.

Byrne read the item again, counted the names and wondered what happened to the name of the third man. But more than that mystery he was taken aback by the governmental announcement. The punishment of hanging for convicted murderers or acts of treason had long been replaced by the use of the electric chair in the state of New York. Now, Byrne was no stranger to brutality. Three times he'd been called to the scene of suicides in the city as a police officer. But one glimpse of a hanging by the neck from a staircase or plumbing fixture, the body loose and discolored, was enough to sour any thoughts of such an end being condoned by a civilized state. He lay the paper down on the bench next to him and conjured the scene of turquoise water and white sand beach. The juxtaposition of such an Eden with three hanging men was difficult to fathom. But a whistle jarred his thoughts: "All aboard, Mr. Byrne," Harris shouted. "Next stop Palm Beach."

Byrne was on the rear apron of the caboose when they started, a perch he favored when they were leaving a place, and he watched Jacksonville disappear. The landscape quickly returned to that of hot, spare pine tree forests and low, prickly-looking scrub vegetation. The train was still gaining speed when Harris joined him.

"Since you've the knack for reading, lad, here's a clipping from early in the week," he said, handing Byrne a folded sheet of newsprint:

Jacksonville, Fla., Feb. 16 — Specials from Titusville, Fla., indicate an alarming state of affairs in the Indian River Country. H.M. Flagler, owner of the Royal Poinciana Hotel on Lake Worth, is building a railroad to the hotel. This road cuts through many of the prettiest places on the Indian River, and thirty of the property owners, it is said, have combined and placed dynamite along the route of the said railway through their lands. These bombs are placed so that they will explode at the stroke of a spade. Signs warning all engineers have been posted, and the property owners have notified the railroad officials of the steps taken. James Holmes, a banker of Jansen, Fla., and J.V. Westen, Tax Collector of Brevard County, have been arrested for complicity in the dynamite plot. Mr. Holmes's lawyer has advised him to remove the dynamite, and it is reported that he has agreed to do so.

Harris watched while the younger man's lips moved. When they stopped Byrne was still staring at the page.

"You know anything about dynamite?" Harris said.

"Blows the hell out of stuff."

"Aye."

"We watched 'em use it when they were building the foundations of the Washington Avenue Bridge," Byrne said. "But not up close,"

"How close?"

"Close enough to hear someone yell 'Fire in the hole!' and then feel the ground move under your feet."

Harris shook his head. "My father, rest his soul, was a miner in the old world," he said. "Explosions every day. While he and his mates ate lunch. Blow the hell out of the ground and turn coal into a chokin' dust.

"Then I seen the results of a stick or two goin' up in the loo of a tavern in Derry. Turned the bar into dust as well."

"Bloody anarchist, were ya?" Byrne said, turning on an accent for the first time and cracking a grin.

"Motivation to leave the mother country," Harris answered. "But these farmers don't know nothin' from dynamite if what it says there is true, and mind you I don't for a minute believe a pinch of what newspapers say. But you can't set it off with the whack of a spade."

"Electric," Byrne said. "From a box."

Harris looked at Byrne for a moment. "You were closer to the Washington Avenue Bridge than you made out to be."

"Sometimes."

"Well, just in case, I'll want you up with the conductor and engineer. Keep those all-seein' eyes of yours out front and let 'em know if you spot any thing that looks suspicious. I already told them to hold down the speed. We're taking the threat seriously, especially when Mr. Flagler is aboard. These folks down here take their land being snaked away from them personally."

Byrne stood and looked into the eyes of his fellow Irishman: "Where don't they take it personally?"

Byrne had not yet ridden in the locomotive and found himself up front on an outrigger step, watching the rails spin out ahead, listening to the pound of engine cylinder and slide of metal, smelling hot grease and burning coal. The engineer and boiler man were rough dressed in canvas dungarees, their clothing stained in soot and coal dust, their brows speckled with sweat. Unlike in the passenger cars, Byrne felt at home, except for the landscape that unfolded one flat mile after the next.

Mile upon mile of pine forests ran to the horizon on the west, with occasional open acres that were stripped of lumber and spread out in tall grasses. On closer inspection, the dark dot-like objects on the distant plain turned into cattle, which he'd never seen anywhere but in the stockyards where the beasts had been penned awaiting slaughter. Recalling the smell and blood of that place caused him to refocus on the tracks in time to pick out a new structure. He called out to the engineer to slow, but the response came as a sneer.

"It's just a siding, boy. For local ranchers and grove owners to use when they're loading," the engineer said. When they came close Byrne could see that the dock-like platform was bare. The weathered wood of the foundation was old work with newer lumber used on top. The new wood brought the ramps up to the level of the train car carriage.

"Used to be a small gauge railroad here till Mr. Flagler bought up the old line and put down standard tracks," the engineer said as Byrne stared at the siding.

"Suppose someone hid underneath and jammed a pipe out into the wheel gear?" Byrne said.

"Ha! She'd shear any piece of metal clean off," said the boiler man. "This engine's pushing two hundred pounds per square inch in a cylinder bigger'n two square feet with each stroke, son. Nobody's goin' to trip her like that."

Byrne nodded, not knowing what the hell the old man meant, but started looking for something more formidable that might be a danger to Mr. Flagler's train. Eight miles east of the small town of Palatka, he found it.

Near the end of a wide, yawning curve in the tracks Byrne again picked up a squared-off blemish in the sameness of the trees and scrub grass lining the way. In the distance he recognized an upcoming siding, but as they came close he could tell that this time there were a number of people on the platform. Closer still, he made them out to be not just field or farm hands, but also women and children. The engineer squinted at the sight himself, an unusual situation that made him pull back on the throttle, taking away the speed that he had already been ordered to cut back on. Less than a quarter mile away someone on the platform began waving a red flag. The engineer applied the brakes.

"You'd best go fetch Mr. Harris," he said to Byrne and then set his jaw. "This ain't right."

Harris was working his way along the walkway alongside the fuel tender with a storm cloud forming in his face.

"No goddamn unscheduled stops," he shouted, but his eyes were looking out on the dozen or so people standing on and about the siding rather than at the train crew.

"You want I should just run over the man and hack 'im into pieces," the engineer said and pointed out through his observation window. In front of the locomotive an elderly man, perhaps in his late fifties, his hair as white as Mr. Flagler's, was standing between the rails, feet spread wide, arms akimbo.

"Christ on a cross!" Harris spat and then said to Byrne as he started down the iron stair, "You're with me."

Byrne scanned the crowd on the platform, level with the train: four men, thin and of average height. The rest women in worn dresses with defiant looks on their faces but either holding protectively onto small children or standing next to boys whose eyes were wide and dancing over the enormity and close metallurgy of the locomotive.

When Harris' feet touched the ground and started moving out toward the man on the tracks, three of the men on the platform started down the platform stairs. Byrne felt the metal wand at his hip but did not touch it. He scanned the men's clothing again, could detect no weapons and moved to a spot halfway between the crowd and where Harris was now confronting the flag bearer.

"I demand to see Mr. Flagler," the man was saying. "I know that his personal car is attached and since he and his railway company have ignored our continued entreaties to end his unfair and despicable takeover of our land and our access to market I demand to confront him in person."

The man was dressed in a worn gray suit, shirt buttoned to the neck despite the heat, and he set his newly shaved chin a few degrees at an upward cant.

Harris folded his huge arms, gripping each elbow and widening his stance. Was he containing his anger, or just building steam to knock the man off the rail bed, Byrne wondered.

"I'm sure you're a fine country lawyer what with your command of the King's English," Harris finally said. "But Mr. Flagler does not meet with anyone without an appointment and he does not answer to demands.

"That said, I'll be pleased to ask you to move yer arse, sir, or I'll have that train plow you under like a bushel of yer own tomatoes."

The lawyer, or farmer, or whoever he was, widened his own stance and crossed his own arms in defiance or in a mock imitation of Harris and the smell of confrontation blew into the crowd, causing all to begin down the platform steps. Byrne again assessed them. These were obviously farmers, the boots under their cuffs stained by the soil, their weathered faces creased by the sun and their forearms cabled with work-hardened muscle. Still, they were nothing like the vicious gang members or violent dock workers he'd dealt with in the city. Nevertheless, he found the handle of his wand with the tips of his fingers.

"*I* surmised that you would be unconvinced," the man said to Harris, his tone unchanged in the face of thousands of pounds of steel and a big Irish tough. "Behind me, sir, is a charge of explosive that upon my signal will be detonated to make these tracks impassible until Mr. Flagler answers to our grievances."

The words caused both Harris and Byrne to slide to the side and peer down the tracks with a more intense scrutiny. Some thirty yards down the line they could make out some form of package that appeared to be wedged beneath the west side rail.

"We have men in control of a device, a plunger if you will, who will not hesitate to blow this train to kingdom come if you attempt to pass."

Byrne watched Harris' back, could see the muscle in the big man's neck start to bulge and the flush of his skin growing redder. Harris seemed to take a deep breath and looked down at the ground. After an anxious moment he turned and began walking back toward the train, his eyes scanning the group of farm families, who had now all gathered at the base of the platform.

When he reached Byrne's side, he winked. The look was not one of resignation or defeat and only made Byrne take a better grip on his baton. The three forward men in the crowd began nodding, muttering their victory, thinking perhaps that Harris was on his way to fetch Flagler. But Byrne had seen Irish like Harris before, men who would never in their lives be trumped on the street by any lawyer, dandy, pimp or bureaucrat.

Turning as the sergeant passed, he watched as Harris shouldered between the three men and then with a quickness that belied his size, he shifted. His hand darted out and snatched the back collar of a boy who had been looking down as Harris walked by, as in deference to an embarrassed adult. Harris then whirled back toward Byrne with the gangly child of some eight years, who was now flailing like a rag doll plucked from a toy chest.

Harris had taken three steps back before the crowd could even react, but with one of their own in peril the three front men began to move to block him. The first man reached out to grab the child but the whoosh and snap of hard thin metal on his forearm stopped all three in their tracks. The stunned man yelped, bent with the pain and folded over at the waist, his now useless arm cradled to his stomach. When Byrne spun the baton a second time, the vibrating sound of air, like the buzz of a giant insect, caused the others to stare at him, seeing the flash of metal for the first time. But with the boy screeching now as Harris dragged him toward the lawyer, one man gathered himself and took another step but was instantly caught by another stroke of Byrne's weapon, this time across the back of the hamstring, which dropped him to his knee. Byrne stepped back, squared himself, let them all see the baton in his hand and spun it wide with a speed that made a few of them gasp.

"You'd best stand where you are, folks. I believe it would be in your interest," Byrne said, not knowing himself whether that was good advice.

He saw that Harris had already pushed the lawyer aside and was heading down the track, dragging the boy behind him, the child's toes tripping on every rail tie. He'd already covered half the distance and called back with a warning that the crowd was only now realizing: "You want to blow one of your children to that kingdom with us, counselor, you'd best get to it."

No one moved except Byrne, who began backing his way down the tracks. The crowd stood mesmerized until a woman, likely the boy's mother, tried to break away but was restrained by the lawyer. On the streets and in the filthy tenements of New York, Byrne had witnessed a dozen acts of self-preservation and utter despair that led hopeless people to sacrifice their children. But these were not those kind of people.

Byrne caught up to Harris' side and looked ahead. Several sticks of dynamite were bound together and wedged under the western rail. A line of sheathed cord ran from the explosives down the embankment and off into a stand of saw palmetto.

"Seen one of these before, lad?" Harris said. The boy he had by the scruff was still wriggling his skinny arms and legs like a pinched snake. But he stopped his squealing when the question was asked, perhaps thinking it had been directed to him, perhaps listening for the answer.

"Yeah. It's a charge that gets blown when whoever's at the end of this cord sends an electric charge through the wire," Byrne said, recalling what he'd seen during the bridge building next to his neighborhood.

All three of them, including the boy, followed the offending cord into the bushes. Harris raised his voice: "And if they wish to blow this little tyke to pieces they can send that current now."

Byrne winced at the bravado. But Harris was right. If they were going to explode their makeshift bomb they'd have done it by now, or simply waited until Flagler's car was directly over it and taken out the train, the track and a dozen passengers.

"They're only here to make a point," Harris said softly. "Which doesn't mean they won't just blow it when we give the kid back."

The boy had been silent till then.

"Maaaawww!" he cried out.

"Couldn'ta said it better myself, boy," Harris said. Then to Byrne: "Do you know how to disarm the damned thing?"

Byrne looked down.

"Best guess, I'd just yank the wire. No electric current, no trigger, like snappin' off the firing pin on your pistol," he said in a voice that made it sound more like a theory than an absolute.

"Fuck then," Harris said. "I'll bring the boy over between you and the bushes and you yank the wire."

Without being able to tell what the men were doing, the farmers and families became restless and started to move up the tracks. Byrne got to his knees, found the charge into which the insulated wire was crammed and pulled it loose, digging the dynamite out from the rail and tucking it under his arm.

"OK. Let's go." He took a step back toward the train. Harris stood still, looking from the explosive pinned next to Byrne's ribs then up into his eyes.

"It's safe?"

"I've seen 'em do it all the time at the bridge," Byrne said.

Harris hesitated for one more beat, then yanked at the boy and followed. When they approached the lawyer, his mouth was loose and hanging slightly open. Nothing came out. Those in the crowd were staring at the package under Byrne's arm. When Byrne climbed up onto the engine rigging, the engineer and fireman aimed their eyes at the same thing and were equally quiet. Harris didn't let go of the boy until he had one foot up on the iron stair and then he shoved the child to the ground toward his crying mother. He raised a thick finger and pointed at the lawyer: "Don't make threats unless you're willing to carry them out, counselor. This ain't no war, sir. It's business."

With that he signaled the engineer to continue forward. As the train began to crawl, Byrne saw two men emerging from the palmetto bushes, their faces up but defeated, their big hands at their sides.

"No more stops," Harris ordered. "We need to get to Palm Beach."

Byrne climbed back over the rigging of the coal car and into the traveling compartments, still a bit dazed by the entire episode. He was working his way toward the back of the train when he realized the sudden gasps of air from some of the passengers and their quick movements to get out of his path were based on the fact that he was still carrying a load of dynamite. When a young mother grabbed her two children and pulled them close, covering their heads with her arms, he looked down at the dark red sticks in his possession: "It won't blow up unless you light it, ma'am."

Still, he took off his jacket and covered the offending package before entering the club car. There were already several men up against the bar, taking some comfort from short glasses of bourbon, and he determined to keep his face down and scuttle on through before anyone asked any questions. But when he looked up to eyeball the rear door he saw that Mr. Faustus was in a corner and was involved in an intense conversation with Mr. McAdams, who Byrne had not seen out of his own coach car since the beginning of the trip. It appeared an intense discussion because Byrne could see the muscles of the old man's jaws flexing, grinding his teeth in some effort of restraint, and the skin of his scalp had turned a shade of red not unlike the color of the dynamite Byrne held in his arm.

McAdams on the other hand was as cool as if he were at a summer social, raising his drink to his lips with profound grace and smoothness while whispering something to Faustus that had struck the older man silent.

CHAPTER EIGHT

MARJORY MCADAMS LEFT THE ROYAL POINCIANA and walked the distance back to the Breakers alone. The heat of midday reached only into the high seventies with the ocean breeze rising. She strode briskly. Those who nodded and smiled their greetings as they passed would have been instead turning their eyes away if they could see the visions she was conjuring in her head: the fire-seared trousers of a dead man, his shirt melted into his charred skin, his body lumped onto the crude lean-to floor like a roll of soft dough settling flaccid without the shape of formed muscle and air-filled lung, and the flame-scarred face with the obscenity of rolled bills protruding from the mouth and that one single eye that had turned a milky white as if the fluid inside had actually boiled. McAdams shivered in the heat, breathed deeply, and extended her stride. She tried again to reconstruct the face as it appeared when the man was alive. And what of the watch? Had Pearson or any of the others noticed that exquisite silver pocket watch the dead man was wearing on a chain attached to his vest? She had seen it. Certainly Pearson would not have missed it.

She spoke only briefly to staff at the Breakers and made her way to her suite, which was oceanfront and on the third floor, which she preferred despite the stairs. The maid was finishing with the bed and was gathering linens. McAdams searched the young woman's face as she had the other workers, looking for pain or some sign of loss.

"Hello, Armie, are you all right?" McAdams said.

"Ma'am?" the girl said.

"I'm sorry, your name is Armie, yes?"

"Yes, ma'am."

"Are you. Excuse me, were you, living in the Styx, Armie, and how did your family fare in the fire?"

"Uh, yes ma'am, I was in the Styx, ma'am, but I ain't got family with me, ma'am."

The girl was younger than McAdams but many of the locals and even women from other parts of the state and beyond followed the work that the trains and resorts had opened for them.

"Do you have someplace to stay, Armie? Someone to stay with?"

"Oh, yes ma'am. Mizz Fleury, she say she already found us a roomin' house on the other side of the lake, ma'am. We gone stay in a big place over near the church on Mr. Flagler's order hisself," the girl said, her chin and voice rising with the use of the man's name as if she was talking of a proud uncle. "Mizz Fleury say Mr. Flagler gone build us our own places in West Palm an ride us to the island ever day for work."

"How nice," McAdams said, but the tone of her voice set the girl to lower her eyes and turn to gather the linens and leave. McAdams did not doubt the rumor. Flagler was noted for innumerable projects he had built along his burgeoning railway. But she had been around wealthy, powerful and paternal men enough to know that there was always a price for their philanthropy. When the girl offered to bring in fresh water for her basin McAdams declined and let her leave.

Alone in the suite McAdams again washed the grit and salt sheen of humidity and sweat off her face and then removed her blouse and did the same for her arms with a sea sponge her father had given her as a present from a place in Florida called Key West. She removed her skirt and sat on the edge of the bed and washed down her legs as well. When she was finished she pulled a sitting room chair over to the double French doors to the balcony and then opened them to the beach and ocean. A salt breeze was blowing in, sweeping back the sheerings of the curtains. She sat and crossed her ankles on a European ottoman, and with the wind brushing the silk of her camisole and her bared legs, she dreamed she was flying.

She was a child in a tree, most likely one of the huge oaks at the family's vacation home in Connecticut. She'd been allowed to climb there, the rules for young ladies and societal appearances be damned in the summertime, said her mother. In the dream she was high in the upper branches and a mist floated under her, obscuring the ground below. She felt frightened and glorious at the same time, the wind in her face, the gauze below and an odd smell of salt in the air though she knew they were nowhere near Nantucket, which was the only place she'd been to smell the sea. She stepped out farther on the limb, standing up but keeping her balance by grasping the thin branches just above. The exhilarating feeling of simply stepping off, spreading her arms and soaring over the familiar grounds of their summer getaway was glowing in her head. But that glimmer of ultimate danger kept her feet in place. She raised her nose to the wind and closed her eyes. The freedom of soaring, or the fear of death? Decide, my dear. You could fly for seconds or for miles. You could fall screaming for fifty feet, or soar forever. She stepped off. The air in her lungs caught in her throat as she went out and down. She was falling, but at the same time hearing a knock at the door, someone assaulting the wood, the noise snapping her awake in midflight.

Marjory's eyes shot open and her hand went immediately to her chest. The knocking was real and shook her awake and she lurched forward, seeing the empty blue sky before her at first and then the horizon, the ocean, the beach, the railing, and finally the floor beneath her.

"My Lord!" she said and caught her breath, closed her eyes and touched her face. Now she distinctly heard the knocking at the door, stood and realized her state of undress. In reaction she brought her spread palms up in a butterfly pattern to cover her exposed breasts.

"Uh, coming!" she called out. "One moment please, I'm not decent!"

When she had draped herself in a housecoat and slipped her shoes back on, she finally went to the front door of the suite and opened it. Before her stood a tall black man, his hat in his hands, the brim pinched between the tips of extremely long and strong fingers. There was a sheen of sweat on his face and he was dressed in the manner of a bellman.

"Yes?" McAdams said, still out of sorts from her dream but her head clearing by the second.

"Excuse me, Miss McAdams. I'm very sorry, ma'am, to disturb you, ma'am. My name is Santos, Carlos Santos. I come to fetch you for Mizz Fleury, ma'am. She needs you to come meet her, please and it's in a hurry, ma'am."

His voice was urgent, his eyes also. McAdams stepped back and took a second accounting. He was a muscular man, one could tell by the squared shoulders, the stretch of fabric over his arms and the V-shape of his chest tapering down into thin hips. McAdams recognized the look and then studied the face, clean shaven and with astonishing green eyes.

"You're the ball player, yes?" she said.

"Uh, yes ma'am."

"I've seen you during the games, the ones with the Cuban Giants that Mr. Flagler displayed out back."

"Yes ma'am," he said again, with no less humility at being recognized.

"If I'm not mistaken, you played third base, yes?"

"Yes ma'am."

"And pitched one game?"

"Yes ma'am."

The baseball games, always played by Negro teams, were organized by the hotel during the winter months and were a favorite among the guests. McAdams had become quite enraptured during the first season that the Royal Poinciana was opened. The Cuban Giants were an especially entertaining team with a group of athletically talented men who seemed unbeatable. Most of the hotel guests knew of course that relatively none of the players were actually from Cuba but played under assumed names so they would be allowed to participate in venues where Negroes were not allowed.

"I believe I saw you hit a home run against a Mr. Sachel Paige," she said, recalling a game from one of those earlier seasons.

"Yes ma'am. Uh, but Mizz Fleury, ma'am, she really needs to see you ma'am," he said, taking a step back as if to draw her out of the room by creating a vacuum.

"Oh, of course," McAdams said, gathering herself. "Right away, Mr. Santos. If you could wait in the lobby, sir. I will be right there."

McAdams dressed in her most conservative black skirt and a ruffled blouse that buttoned high on her neck. She supposed the clothes she selected were in response to the fact that she had been in such a mode of undress when Mr. Santos was just outside her apartment door. She rolled her hair and tucked it up under a straw hat and went downstairs.

Santos was just near the entryway. She went directly to him and again he drew her outside by backing his large, muscular body away. Not seeing Miss Fleury, she looked questioningly into the black man's eyes.

"She's in the laundry, ma'am," he answered the unasked question. "She's holding someone there and can't come herself, but she needs you."